STREET NURSES

BY

Alvin Williams & Tammy Williams

Printed by Tammy'Dele Book Publishing, LLC., in the United States of America.

First printing, 2020.

Tammy'Dele Films Book Publishing, LLC

461 Sandy Creek Road

Suite 1143

Fayetteville, GA 30214

www.TammyDeleBookPublishing.com

ISBN 978-164316559-2

About the Authors

Tammy Williams

Thanks for stopping by! My career in television kicked off after my third internship turned into a real, paying job in the news department at WTVF-TV (CBS) in Nashville, TN over 25 years ago. With critical deadlines, I learned to edit fast and deliver efficiently. I caught the creative bug and decided to pursue my desire to write and produce commercials. The Promotion/Marketing Department at WRCB-TV (NBC) in Chattanooga was an exciting time as I wrote and produced station image spots and news and entertainment promos. My next stop was WDSU-TV (NBC) in New Orleans as a Writer/Producer in the Promotion/Marketing Department. Daily new topicals, station image, and entertainment promos were my main areas, later adding long-formatted and live shows to my portfolio.

I am a storyteller and I have translated that creative ability into narrative features, documentaries, and biographies. On the technical side of production, I hire and manage multi-camera crews as well as smaller teams. I manage producers and work as a post-production supervisor. Feel free to read more details about my production journey at tammydelefilms.com. Thanks for stopping by!

Alvin Williams

Alvin V. Williams is currently, a Writer, Producer, and Educator for Tammy'Dele Films. Williams' current productions include The Chronicles of Ernie and Cerbie, Dempsey The Dog, Rescue Sal, and Whistle Blower.

Williams is the former Executive Vice President and co-founder of Alchemy Networks, developing a new digital to TV model targeted to the 13 to 34 multicultural millennials and 25 to 54 women of color. Alvin was responsible for marketing, business development, publicity, online, social media, and ad sales.

Williams' tenure also includes a post as Senior Director of Music, Talent & Acquisitions at UP TV, where he was instrumental in launching the small cable network from zero households to over 40 million households as Director of Affiliate Marketing & Affinity Promotions. Alvin was later tapped by the CEO to create the Music Industry & Acquisitions department that lead to the success of advertiser supported short-form and long-form programming, the creation of Gospel Play, and acquisition of a wide range of programming for the network.

Williams is also a former A&R director, first with Word Entertainment/Warner Brothers, where he was responsible for signing and executive producing projects for artists such as Shirley Caesar, Marvin Sapp, The WOW project, and others. Williams also created and was Director of Music Word Gospel/Sony Music. A&Red projects and worked with artists such as Beyonce, Kelly Rowland, Michelle Williams, and MTV/Paramount Pictures movie, The Fighting Temptations. Under William's direction, his first release with Michelle Williams entered the Gospel Billboard charts at #1 as well as his second release, debut at #1, The soundtrack to The Fighting Temptations.

He holds a B.A. in Business Administration from Tennessee State University and is an honorably discharged veteran of the United States Army.

TABLE OF CONTENTS

CHAPTER 1

The increasing pain had her wilting. She hugged her knee tightly knotting her legs between her hands, desperate to ease her pain. But each drift and movement struck hard at her senses doing nothing to relieve her of the hard tingle she felt from her bruised skin. Fingers twitched to each cringle of resonating pain, her eyes rolled. she could barely feel her arms as her face was sore and unbearably hot.

She tilted her head. It was hard to, the skin was crisp, the air was dry. Her lips parted just for a brief second to release the air stagnant in the pit of the throat, threatening to choke her. She coughed, choking on her own spit. Slobbering the slim contents down the side of her small mouth, she breathed out and tried hard to compose her stiff body.

She was hurting all over, and she still craved for a fix. She wanted just a fix. That was all she wanted.

How did I end up like this?

She spat out some blood and rolled over, the pain traveled fast like lightening, coursing through every part of her body. She fidgeted and tried to think happy thoughts, she read somewhere that they help take your mind off the pain. Her happy thoughts were thoughts of her mother, her smile, how she would drive her to never give up.

But here I was giving up…

Brianna couldn't get up even if she tried. She was in excruciating pain and this was compounded by the reality that she had no money. She thought, he had always given her loan for heroin but why did he suddenly lose his temper and lash out on her?

Damn it, I shouldn't have come here in the first place. Now I will die here.

Even now, she knew she was badly injured. She was bleeding from too many places. Injuries to the mouth, she spat out more blood. She knew she was in a pool of her own blood; she could see it from the corner of her eyes. She winced at the sight. She could never have spat out that much. Her head felt like it was on fire. She could barely feel her legs, they were tense. Her right ankle suffocated with pain from the kick it received while he was slamming it against the brick wall.

The tarmac was cold, she needed help but how could anyone help her if they couldn't even find her? Brianna tried to move her head again but a sharp pain to her neck instructed her otherwise. Should she risk it? Brianna knew screaming for help could get her someone, but she also knew it could get her in trouble. She groaned in frustration. In this dark alley, no one would come to her rescue.

The night sky just beyond the tall roof was inviting. The darkness always seemed like that. It would call out to you. It knew your secrets. It knew how to entice you. It knew hers, heroin. She was addicted to it; she came here just for that but she had no money. The darkness swallowed her up in anger.

Brianna had taken solace in heroine after she lost her mother who was her only remaining family and doubled as her best friend in the whole world. They always had their differences, she wasn't too happy that her mother always had to work, leaving her all by herself. But she always said, "she had to do it for those who had nobody," whatever that meant. Her mother worked with the city hospital as a nurse, but unlike other nurses who had time off, her mother seemed to work round the clock. Brianna had never understood why that was. She just concluded her mother was trying to get away from her and her teenage excesses.

A sharp pain to her side jolted her back to her present condition. She was bleeding out.

Mom, if you can hear me, please I need help.

At least the stars were out. They kept shining bright, in spite of her now blurry vision. She felt calm even as her breathing got shallow. A light shone brightly and moved across her vision.

Brianna clammed up.

"Damn, hope we are not too late…"

That voice, it sounded familiar. Something formed around her arm, it was cold but it swiftly got warm. Tingling lightly to the cracked skin, Brianna shook uncontrollably.

"We need to move."

Brianna heard the voice command. She strained to catch a grip of whose voice it was, the voice brought such tranquility that felt so familiar. She wanted to know the source but she could not shake the pain. It was all-consuming. It threatened to destroy her. She feared it was too late, she felt she screwed up, Brianna thought she really did. All of sudden her body was wrapped, arms, fingers of warm hands cradled her body and lifted her.

Something soft ribbed into her back, she shook. Eyes desperate for an explanation, try as much as she could, she could not decipher the blurs. She only saw the stars blinking thinly yet brightly.

She drew in a long breath and exhaled her last breath as if it was a dim consequence. Shuddering she lost all feeling.

CHAPTER 2

Ping

Ping

What was that sound? Brianna shuddered for a while then she realized she could think. Was this a dream? She could not see anything. She tried to open her eyes but some force was dragging it shut.

She tried to fight it; her body stiffened as she threw her head back. Breathing out, she let out a gasp. Her eyes ripped open, light blue roof. Was that a metal pole? She turned her weary eyes towards it.

A bag of saline hung on the pole, beyond that was a white sheet. It was an IV. She looked on wondering if she was really in a hospital and how she got there.

"Brianna,"

That voice. Brianna looked forward, but the hand gripped her on her left arm. Brianna's eyes followed up the arm to ogle at Angelic. Angelic was her mother's old friend. Both were nurses and Angelic was pretty much her Godmother. Brianna could not believe it. Brianna could not form the words, hell, her lips gaped open pondering what she should do next. How did she end up in a hospital with Angelic? She felt embarrassed, she hated that Angelic had to see her in this pitiful state.

Angelic patted her on the arm, "Try to calm down," she had motioned at the heart monitor and her heightened heart rate. "You have been through a lot, just rest."

Her voice was calming, like still waters. Angelic had always had this calmness about her. The sort of peace that told you she was not judging whatever you had done, but was there to help you.

Brianna was tired, it was hard to keep her eyes from fluttering shut. The more she wanted to sleep, the more the pain reminded her of what had happened to her. She was badly beaten up by her dealer. She rolled her eyes at the irony of someone actually saving her life, if he finds out she was alive she does not have his money he will kill her.

Brianna groaned at her future prospects as she noted the rather stark room. This white sheet was all around her. The floor was clean but it expanded beyond the white fence that was put up. Actually, what held the white sheet was a metal pole, she could barely see the sheen.

The trolleys were arranged but quite oddly. It was not the way she would expect it to be. On top was a kidney dish with a splash of betadine still left inside.

Brianna peeked a look at the rails of her bed, rusty, peeled paint. At least it was clean or looked clean, she was not sure if the workers here were that diligent.

She had to ask, "Where am I, what crummy hospital is this?"

Angelic giggled, her plum gray hair twisted in round bangs on the sides. "You always paid close attention to detail. Just like your mother."

Brianna groaned as the pain seemed to increase with every breath taken. She shook on the bed. Brianna sneered, "Don't remind me of her now. I just-"

"She built this place actually."

Brianna looked directly into Angelic's somber yet peaceful eyes. Angelic whispered almost, "This place was built with your mother's hands. Try to have a little bit more respect for it."

"She…had a hospital?" Brianna knew her relationship with her mother in her last days wasn't superb, but she didn't think she could keep something as big as owning a hospital from her, at least this looked like one.

Angelic laughed again. "No," Angelic looked away. "This is a private clinic. The Street Nurses is what we called it. We help anyone that can't go to a traditional hospital, maybe because of insurance, drug addiction, criminal or any other reason," She added, beaming with a sense of pride.

Brianna stared at Angelic like she was mad. Brianna looked around and pondered sternly what she just heard. It was hard to believe and yet here she was.

Still, Brianna was confused, a part of her admired her mother's philanthropy, but the other part that knew what was right and wrong under the long was upset. Why would her mother do such a thing? She had always known her mother was a bit extra when it came to helping people, but this felt like a step too far. Not only was it risky, but it was also illegal. Also, how long has this been doing on?

Why did her mother not say anything about this all this while? Brianna groaned as a pain hits her in the head. As if a monster was peeling off her skin, the pain was riveting and tense to her every move and mood.

The rapid beep of the machine sent her mind whirling as if the pain she felt was in sync with the beeping sound.

"Brianna, calm down, breathe in, breathe out. Just be still, calm down." Angelic gripped her hand tightly and tried to calm her. Brianna was still shell-shocked. She fluttered her eyes briefly before rolling her head to the other side.

Pushing out long breaths burdened with her distress, Brianna muscled up the resolve to at least still her wild mind.

"Yes, just breathe Brianna," Angelic echoed, her voice a bit distant in Brianna's head.

"Angelic, when did all this happen? How come she never mentioned it to me?" She couldn't get over the reality that her mother couldn't confide in her concerning this obviously huge part of her life.

"Ah, come now, just rest I will answer your questions later when you feel better."

Brianna shot her a glare. "If something is about to alter my life forever, I would rather hear it now than later."

Angelic laughed nervously. "I wouldn't call this is life-altering…"

"Angelic all those years I could barely see my mother, the late nights, the dinners she forgot to cook because she was always in a hurry. The breakfast she did not make. I always thought she just hated being at home. Brianna snorted, then she laughed a peal of weak laughter. Coughing at the end, it frightened Angelic but Brianna held up her hand to show that she was fine.

Brianna continued, "All this time she was here?"

"She worked at a hospital different from working here. But she spent most of her time here, especially during her last days. She always liked helping people. She hated how the hospitals treated people. She hated the moral compass they wielded so hypocritically." Angelic said that with poised disgust.

Brianna wanted to be a nurse herself. She never knew much about the inside environment she never even got a chance to. Brianna dropped out, a failure. She wanted to be just like her mother and yet she failed, and when she did, she couldn't take the hit that came with the pressure of her loss. She took it out on her mother, picking a fight with her at every turn because she was barely around, but when her mother became sick and couldn't work anymore, she felt her world crumble.

I should be ashamed, my mother was working two jobs, put herself at risk of going to jail and I could not even survive college? Pathetic…

"My mother was always so super. Anyways, this is cool. I get to live again because of something she created." Brianna finally said to Angelic.

Angelic shot her a narrowed look. She shifted as she looked like she was measuring Brianna up. "You say that like you are not happy."

Brianna widened her eyes and shook her head. "No, it ain't cause I hate my mom or anything. I just miss her is all Angelic, I just…"

"Who did this to you, Brianna?"

Brianna snorted, and spat out, "A dude." Brianna surmised she would need a new link.

Angelic moved closer. "What, you need to stop dating that guy! Who beats up thei-"

Brianna was laughing hard, slamming her arm on the bed. "Calm down Angelic, it is not my boyfriend. I don't even have one. It is my dealer. A dealer, he is a dealer, a heroin dealer…I wanted heroin. I did not have any money and I owed him. Thought he would have helped me out but…damn nearly killed me. Almost killed me…"

Angelic drew back, hands on her quivering lips. "Oh my god, sweety, y-you are addicted to heroin?"

"Ya, I am. I wish I could beat it; I wish I could turn back the clock but I can't. It has a hold on me Angelic. It jus-"

She grabbed Brianna much to her shock. Her arms swept around Brianna's broken body, causing the pain to travel through the deep crevices of her skin, but Brianna did not mind.

She had not been hugged in ages. All the friends she had never gave her one, they only ask for money, a needle or a shot.

"Don't worry, we will get you cleaned up. I promise. I swear on your mother's grave you will beat this. We will beat this, together," Angelic said, still holding her in the warm embrace.

Brianna closed her eyes, tears flowed onto Angelic's scrubs as her mind finally felt at peace. She fell asleep, the star over her life still bright.

CHAPTER 3

If anyone told Brianna her lifestyle could get her killed, she would have probably cussed them out or picked a fight with them, pretending she didn't know it was possible. But she lived a really rough life back then. She almost did die.

Things have changed over the last few years. Brianna had put in so much work into becoming a better version of herself while trying hard to cut ties with what almost killed her. It was a hard transition but Brianna was doing better than she ever thought she would. Nothing was too tough for her right now; she knew people had it worse. Since she got clean she decided she was going to spend her life helping the ones that fell through the cracks who didn't know there was a way out.

Brianna would show them that way out if she could, "You need to stop smoking, or that cough of yours isn't going to go away," She tells the homeless man she is examining.

The man grumbled, "I can't just quit. It's not that simple."

Brianna slid the stethoscope back unto her neck. She could relate to his struggle more than he knew. She knew all too well but she defeated that battle and was standing before him clean. She looked at him and said, "I know it's hard to break an addiction. Trust me. But if you want a better life, this is how you start."

The man acknowledged what she said with a nod, but she knew he didn't agree.

"Plus, just think of all the money you'd have if you didn't spend it on smokes. Maybe you wouldn't have to be out here anymore.

The homeless man almost laughed looking at her. He nods, "Maybe you're right."

"I know I am."

She decided to put her stethoscope back in her bag. "Anything else bothering you?"

"No, just the coughing," The homeless replied as he stood up, "Thank you. I don't know what I, we'd, do without you," He said amidst coughs.

Yes, it had become a routine for her and her team to come to the streets and check on the homeless and unfortunate. All of them knew her and she could hardly walk one block without someone calling out to her, just to say 'hi' or 'good morning.'

Brianna loved every moment she spent being a Street Nurse, not because her mother was one. But because she was genuinely helping people without reservations and rules, she was helping everybody.

Brianna could now see why her mother enjoyed this line of work. It was the work of angels that descended from the sky forgoing their worldly duties to be of service to mankind. It felt like that to her to some extent.

Brianna smiled deeply and replied, "It's my pleasure." She began to walk away but did leave one piece of advice for him while he was still in earshot. "Promise me you'll find a way to quit those death sticks."

"I'll find a way." The man replied, almost shouting.

Brianna smiled as she held her head high while exiting the ally.

She walked toward an unmarked black van. Brianna looked around to make sure no one was watching her. She opened up the van's passenger side door and got into the van.

"How's he doing?" Malvin one of her colleagues asked as she got in.

Malvin is also a nurse and has become an essential part of the team. He graduated from community college with good grades and wanted to do more than just saving lives for a paycheck. He was pretty determined and hard-working when it came to assisting Brianna in her mission. Mary-Jane was the connection that brought him here.

She met him at a hospital she used to work for. According to Mary-Jane, he was the only one that was not a cork in the system there. Even though he did not talk very much, Mary-Jane noticed that unlike other nurses who viewed nursing as just another job or a source of income, Malvin embraced it as a calling to really serve humanity.

Her spirit took to him she said. Brianna almost laughed thinking about it. She had never seen anyone as empathetic and genuinely concerned about people as Malvin.

She smiled just thinking about their meeting.

Malvin cocked an eyebrow "What's up?" he asks, a puzzled look on his face.

"Nothing," Brianna looks to the back of the van. There's nobody there. An empty stretcher sits idle.

"How is he doing," Malvin asked.

She shut the door.

"The coughing is getting worse. He needs to quit smoking if there is a chance that cough would stop, but it's really his choice what he wants to do."

"Where's Adele?" Brianna asked, looking around.

"She should be back any second. She wanted to grab a bite to eat," Malvin replied.

"We're not late to any calls, are we?" Brianna asked just to make sure.

"No, nothing's come in, yet."

Brianna breathed out and laid back. She was always on edge; such was the job. She and Malvin were full-time Street Nurses. Keeping the services, they rendered going was not only time consuming but also cost money. The only way they could afford it was through a sponsor they met through their contact Mary-Jane.

Adele was also their colleague; a fellow street nurse. Meeting Adele was a weird coincidence. She used to work at the city hospital where Brianna's Mom once worked. Just like Angelic and her mother Adele was not impressed with how people were treated in the hospital, especially people who didn't have enough money or health insurance. So, when Angelic offered her a position as a street nurse, she was ecstatic. Brianna knows all of her excesses, especially her love for money and monetary gains, but she was still thankful for her and the fact that she was always available to take calls. After all, everyone has their own flaws, Brianna thought to herself as she stretched.

She wouldn't really blame any of them for trying to hustle a little bit more; the money they get paid was not much. But it helps and it really does make their efforts worthwhile. Brianna wasn't really bothered about the income. As far as she was concerned, and from how she was brought up by her parents, helping others came first.

"I hope we don't get any dangerous calls," Malvin blurted out, snapping her out of her thought.

"Why, because they are dangerous?"

"No, because I know you."

Brianna laughed. "Sounds like you know me too well."

"Of course, I do, you would jump to go do any call without hesitation. You…are braver than I could ever be," Malvin complimented her, looking out the window as he spoke.

"I am not," Brianna answered, her eyes still fixed on the road as she kept watching the cars drive by. The bustling activities interested her; people walking briskly to their destination, some walking leisurely totally oblivious to the rush, which was symbolic of the world's complacency. Nobody stopped for a minute to look toward these alleys or any of its residents. No good mornings were exchanged between people as they walked by. "I just want to help everyone I guess."

"I always imagined myself being this hero when I started working here."

Brianna gave Malvin a glance cocking her brow. "Really?"

"I mean yeah, it sounded like that to me when Mary-Jane brought the idea to me. It really appealed to me."

Brianna acknowledged him with a nod. She understood what Malvin felt. "People look up to us you know, it is a good feeling."

"Almost like a dr-"

"Drug?" Brianna finished.

Malvin held out his palms as he pleaded. "So, sorry, I did not mean fo-"

Brianna cut him off. "Don't worry about it. I have been down that road a long time ago. That is over and done with." Malvin felt a sense of relief wash down his body at the realization that she knew he didn't mean to remind her of the past. Brianna smiled as she watched the world outside. "The thing about life is that you always need something to latch onto. Something to devote your life towards, a purpose, that is what you need to make life fulfilling. With drugs, it gave me purpose when I lost my mother."

Malvin opened his mouth but Brianna stared at him pointedly, "Street Nurses is my new purpose now."

Malvin nodded, "Without your mother and Angelic, this would not be possible."

"Yes, indeed. I am glad, now it is my, no our turn to continue their legacy." Brianna looked out the door window. "Which reminds me where is Adele?" She is taking an awfully long time."

CHAPTER 4

Inside the deli, at the small storefront were small bar-shaped sandwiches under the glass enclosure. Standing amongst the stiff crowd was Adele. She is wearing a black blouse, blue skirt with black lines coursing at sharp angles at the sides, tall black socks, and a pointed mouth shoe. Her blond hair hung low and swept her head in a circle as her slightly pale skin glowed from the little ray of sun that sipped into the Deli through the window. She is waiting for her order. Rocking back and forth in growing impatience, she fiddled her fingers in anticipation. The deli worker wrapped the sandwich, placed it into a brown paper bag. He called out the order number. "Number seventy-three. Seventy-three."

Adele looks down at her receipt, number seventy-three. She steps forward and grabs the bag, flashing an irritated smile.

Adele began to walk briskly towards the door.

"Ma'ma!"

She heard someone call out, but did not assume it was her, not like she left her change or anything.

"Ma'ma! Nurse!"

Adele stopped in her track and turned. She was agitated but she put on a plastic smile to hide her obvious irritation. A man with a heavy beard was approaching her. The man looked relatively respectable in his gray suit. He shivered a lot, his eyes seemed too striking. Adele was not unnerved. Though those old dusty white sneakers were distracting considering the attire, Adele ignored that and asked, "What can I do for you?"

"You're a nurse, right?" he asked.

"That's why I stopped."

"Do you have any Oxycontin on you?"

Adele looked at him stupefied for a second. Adele wanted to look around her and see if someone was listening in on their conversation. Adele gritted her teeth in frustration. She was peeved to bother.

"Are you serious?" She blurted out hoarsely.

The man came closer. "Yes, I am serious."

"It's only for people who are seriously in need of it," Adele blurted out, shooting him a suspicious look.

"Oh, I need it."

Adele rolled her eyes and turned around. She h for the door.

"I've got money."

Adele stopped. She knew she really had to leave. But she might not get another chance to get some payday since Adele took the last call. It was now Brianna's turn, Adele begrudgingly thought. Adele sighed and slowly turned around.

"I think I need to use the bathroom," Adele said. She shot a glare at him then looked away as she passed him. She hoped he got the message because she was not in the mood to create a scene right here.

"Oh!" he said as he trailed behind her. Adele almost sighed, she could guess he got it.

Adele entered the bathroom and the Nervous Guy followed. He shut and locked the door behind him.

"How much?" he asked.

"How much you got?" she retorted aggressively.

The Nervous Guy reached into his pocket and pulled out a wad of cash. He hands it over to her.

She quickly counted the money. Over a hundred dollars, she hurriedly dropped the money in her sandwich bag.

She reached into her pocket and pulled out a prescription bottle. She took off the lid and poured out a couple of pills.

She handed them to the man, he stared down at the pills in his open palm, looked at her with a frown and asked, "That's it?"

Adele flexed her jaw and coldly offered, "I can take them back."

"No, no. This is fine."

"You didn't get them from me."

"Of course."

She shoved the man as she opened the door and walked away.

"Thanks!" He bellowed out after her. Through the sliver of vision, she saw eyes hit her as she was exiting. *The least he could do was shut up and exit quietly but no, shout it loud for everyone to hear.* She promised to hit him anytime their path crossed.

She hurried across the street. Adele steps into the van. Malvin and Brianna quickly turn around when they noticed the presence in the van, but on seeing Adele they both relax. Adele sits down about to dig into her lunch.

"There you are. What took so long?" Malvin was the first to ask.

Adele thinks for a moment. "Ran into an old friend," she took out the sandwich. "And you know how slow those guys in the deli are."

A phone rings. Malvin reaches for it.

Another job probably, Adele thought. It was not often but sometimes they would get work from confidential contacts that knew about their organization. It was supposed to be a secret but with so many people knowing about them, Adele wondered how long it would be until the government found out. She was even surprised it hadn't happened yet.

"Hello?" Malvin answers.

Adele had no problem with it, actually, it was better. The ones that called were likely people who could not go to a hospital because they were trying to avoid the police or had no insurance. At least they usually had money, the other work which was checking on homeless people was nice but afforded no extra money other than her usual pay.

The house visits only paid a commission from the donation to anyone who answers the calls. At least that is what Angelic called it, it mattered little what it was called. As long as it was money, she was game.

Adele believes going public would pay them more, but on second thought, they'd probably be thrown into jail. She shoved a piece of her sandwich into her mouth. The tomato slushed with the smooth melted cheese and the hot sting of the beef.

Brianna tries listening to the conversation.

Malvin got a determined look on his face. "We'll leave right now. We'll be there in a few minutes."

Adele rolled her eyes. She had always thought of Malvin as being too desperate to impress. *Who says a few minutes?* They were probably on the other side of town for all she knew. It was not her time yet so she did not care.

Malvin hung up the phone.

"What is it?" Brianna asked sounding worried.

"Young boy was riding his bike and crashed it. His mother said he might have broken his leg."

Malvin turned on the ignition. He put the van in drive and began to steer the vehicle out of the parking space.

"How far away?"

"A few miles."

"Drive safely," Brianna said.

Adele almost laughed. The van began to speed down the street.

Malvin looks Rambo behind that wheel. Man, I swear Malvin actually trying to make that 'few minute' projections come true. This, I have to see.

Adele sucked the sauce off her thumb. If they get a ticket it would be Malvin's first brush with the law. Adele snickered. She knew what they were doing was illegal, but she also knew it was necessary. The official system of healthcare was nothing more than a big scam. Adele has worked long enough for these fat cats to know they had no ends to their moral manipulation.

She would rather work as a street nurse and actually do something good than work for some hospital administrator who covered as much ass as they kissed it. The paycheck they get must pay for a lot of lipstick. Adele hated makeup and that is what they wore, makeup.

Lying while writing down patient death records when a doctor makes a mistake, bowing before donors like some indentured servants. Adele hated them. Working on that measly salary and all those heavy hours, it was hard on her back then.

Adele took another big bite from her sandwich which was almost forgotten. Adele was in a better place now. With the Street Nurses, she felt more at home than she ever did anywhere else. Plus the money was not bad.

CHAPTER 5

Brianna shielded her eyes from the daring glare of the encroaching sun. Malvin walked past her as he headed toward the front door, a medical bag strapped to his bag.

It was a blue house with brown shingles. A driveway was gated and the over brush of leaves and flowers from the tree guarded a bicycle against the heat.

Malvin waited, Brianna came up behind him and nodded to him as a signal.

The door opened. A woman was standing before them. She had ashy brown hair and blue eyes. She smiled and clutched her hands together anxiously.

"Are you guys, the…Street Nurses?" she asked.

Brianna smiled at that. It was not often they were called that. Even though that was the name of their team and organization, it was not like they wore matching shirts or anything. Most people did not really know their name, they just knew that her team could help. Luckily that was all that mattered to her and her team.

She nodded, "Yes we are. Where's the boy?"

The woman quivered, "In the living room. Thank you, guys, for coming. I didn't know what else to do. Follow me."

Brianna and Malvin followed closely as she led the way. Brianna's eyes instantly caught sight of who they had come to see. A young boy, probably around ten, laid on the couch. His face looked twisted as he rolled continuously on the couch in obvious pain.

His mother stooped close to his head and whispered, "Honey, the people are here, ok? They are going to look at you, alright?"

Brianna noticed he was grabbing the calf of his left leg. Is that where the injury is? It might be bad Brianna thought.

The woman looked back at Brianna. "Please can you help him?"

Brianna walks over to the Young Boy with a warm smile on her face. "Hello. I'm Brianna and I'm going to help you. Your mom says your leg hurts."

"Yes." The boy replies visibly shaking from trying to hold in the tears.

"You're a pretty tough kid," Brianna says, noticing that he was trying to keep it together.

The boy smiles through the pain.

Malvin places the medical bag down. Unzips the bag, pulls out a pair of gloves, he hands the gloves to Brianna.

Brianna puts on the gloves and kneels beside the boy. "I'm going to take your pants off, so I can get a better look at your leg, okay?"

"Okay."

Brianna pulls down his pants, leaving him only with his boxers. She examines his leg. There are a few scratches but nothing looks severe. Maybe the issue is in the bone Brianna wondered. "I'm going to touch your leg and you let me know if it hurts when I touch it, okay?"

The boy nods.

Brianna starts to press different areas of his leg. She presses by his shin.

The boy almost sat up screaming, "Ouch. There. That hurts."

"And that's the only place that hurts?" Brianna asked.

"Yes."

"Okay."

Brianna looks up at Malvin. She gives him a concerned look.

Malvin stared up at the mother and asked, "Can we talk alone for a minute?"

She looked horrified, but she nods, "Sure."

Malvin and the Mother step out of the room.

"You're doing great. I'm going to put your leg in a splint. It'll hurt just a little, but it'll keep you from moving your leg and hurting it more."

The Young Boy takes a deep breath as Brianna straightened his leg on the couch.

"Okay," Brianna uttered before reaching into the medical bag. She pulls out the supplies she'll need. Brianna could tell his shin was broken. Malvin could see it for himself as well. She did not want to say it in front of the boy. He had been really brave and she didn't want to risk taking away that brave smile. He probably thought this was going to be a small hindrance like a simple finger cut.

Brianna would think the same thing too if she did not know any better. She thought of how it felt to be young again, but she shook the carefree thoughts out of her mind and focused on getting this tape slid over his leg. She already slid two thick pieces of board on either side of his leg. The tape was firmly wrapped to tighten and grip his leg. He winced with each roll rounding his leg. This setup would prevent the bones from moving around too much and causing him more injury.

Bones were strong but they can be fickle when broken and on the verge of breaking. Brianna wished they could help but this was beyond their overall skill. That and the fact that Mary-Jane was not very good with bones recuperation. She was more of an Emergency Response doctor.

Still, Brianna hoped the mother would take her son to help. Granted what she and the others could do was a great service to the community. But they could only do so much. Brianna really wanted to help everyone but that wouldn't be possible with the limited resources they had.

The hospitals may be a cruel place with exorbitant fees and costs that the masses couldn't afford, but the resources they had meant they could cover and assist with almost any treatment for any ailment.

A power that was protected by law, Brianna and her team were skirting a thin line.

Brianna was now finished and patted his leg. "All done, you will be fine for now."

Malvin and the mother walked back into the living room.

"Is he allergic to any medication?" Brianna asked the mother.

"No."

Brianna takes out a bottle from the bag and drops a pill into her hand. She hands the pill to the boy. "That'll help with the pain."

"Thank you, guys, so much," his mother said her face plastered with worry.

"That's why we're here, but the pain relief is only temporary."

She shook her head. "I understand."

Brianna grabs the bag as she stands.

The mother comes closer, "What do I owe you guys?"

Malvin waves his hand nonchalantly. "Whatever you can spare."

"Wait right here," she said.

Talking softly so the boy doesn't hear them, Brianna asked, "What did you tell her?"

"That he needs to go to a hospital. The break might be more severe than what we can handle," Malvin answered.

"What did she say?"

"She said she'd take him."

Brianna heaved a sigh of relief. "Good."

The Mother rejoined them. She hands them some money. "There's about a hundred there. I've been saving up. That's all I can afford."

"That's more than enough. That'll make it possible for us to go help the next person," Brianna replied.

The mother gave a knowing smile. "We'll show ourselves out," Malvin said as they turned to leave.

Brianna and Malvin walked out of the room.

Brianna heard the woman say to her son, "You're going to be more careful next time, right?" Brianna smiled as she exited the house. The sun kept up its assault on her bland skin.

Brianna went around the back as Malvin opened the driver seat door. Adele was startled awake and straightened as Malvin sat beside her. "You sleeping so early in the morning?" Melvin laughed nudging her slightly.

Adele snorted. Then she slurred as she waved her hand, "Please tell me we are going back?"

"That depends, we got any calls?"

"No."

Malvin smirked his face slightly rough on the edges as he stared down at her. "How would you know if you were sleeping?"

"I was not sleeping, I had my eyes closed, that is all."

"Oh, so you were meditating?"

Brianna snickered. "Funny Malvin, just go," Adele snapped

"Alright, alright, let me call Angelic and tell her we are coming in," Malvin said.

They moved off and were soon on the road. Brianna took some time to nap. She was tired. They were all tired, and it was no surprise because their job had no fixed hours and a lot of people needed help. They were the only ones in this city doing the work they were doing. So they got a lot of calls and naturally, all-nighters were often.

It was almost like a hospital. Brianna probably wouldn't know so much, she was a grad student with little experience with real hospitals. Her only experience was the Memorial Hospital close to the college and they did go on field trips there to just give those students a bird's eye view of what it was like in a hospital.

She wanted to be a nurse just like her mother. Her mother had been through so much to keep this organization. Brianna exhaled and tried to calm her mind. She had struggled really hard with coping with the reality that her mother was dead.

Brianna was not going to let the pain of her loss stop her stride. She knew her mother would have wanted her to keep pushing. She wouldn't let herself fall like she did before. She had to break the cycle. Brianna had to do better and strive for a better world.

She felt like she could do it with just her hands. Her mother always said it takes one person to change the world.

CHAPTER 6

"…she looks so…"

"Like you look any better, you got bags under your eyes!..." Brianna could not decipher the voice as her thoughts raged on where she was. Brianna opened her eyes slowly and peered through the blurriness. The dim dull metal wall of the van greeted her.

"Ah, caught you slipping girl!" Brianna turned to Adele who was smiling at her. Adele then laughed as Brianna leaned up.

"Guess you did," Brianna said. They exited the van in the star-sprinkled night and before them was an old apartment building. Derelict, the paint was heavily peeled in many places. Graffiti, faded and sprayed all over in a confusing language. The wall was thick with smut in some places, torn flyers on the lower sections. Broken off chips of concrete from acid rain or mishaps, the place looked abandoned.

Well, it probably was condemned. Brianna was not completely sure. Still, it was not that bad; it could be still fixed up. A little paint could brighten this place up.

But it was better this way. Its rough outer look was the perfect cover for what was inside: Their operation. They stepped in. The first floor was filled with two decrepit couches and a mahogany wood front desk that still looked good even with the dust. They stepped past the desk and went into the side office. Malvin pushed back this smaller desk. He grabbed the side of the carpet and revealed the large trap door underneath. Brianna, Malvin, and Adele walked down the sloping decline into the basement.

It was not completely dark. Opening the door turned on the lights on the roof. The room they entered had steel walls. With a more refined finish and aseptic smell that reminded her that this was more familiar territory. Across from the room were two big swivel doors.

Brianna pushed open the basement doors. They all enter. Another door greets them. Beside this door, a keypad lock. Brianna enters the code. The door unlocks. They enter.

The basement room was large and was brightly lit. Two corridors led to different sides of the building. Everything is very clean. Which was important to prevent infection, they lived with a constant reminder that there was a quite unsanitary world above them.

In the center of the room was a half-circle of a desk, they walked over to that desk where Angelic, was sitting.

"Angelic. How's everything going?"

"Everything's been calm. Nothing to report. Only one new patient." Angelic hands Brianna a folder. "Going through heroin withdraw."

Brianna always paused when she heard the word Heroin. Well, she knew about heroine from experience, she was the best person to deal with this. Brianna had to be brave every time she was faced with Heroin or dealing with a patient undergoing withdrawal.

Brianna nodded as she turned to Adele and Malvin.

"Why don't you guys go get some rest. I'll be up in a few minutes."

"You sure that's a good idea? You've been up as long as we have?" Malvin asked.

"I'll be fine. I'm just going to introduce myself to the new patient. I'll join you in a few minutes."

Malvin gives in and nodded in agreement. Malvin and Adele headed back upstairs.

Brianna turned back to face Angelic. "Where is she?"

"Room three."

Brianna walked toward the corridor to the left, which led to the surgery and recovery rooms. Brianna navigated herself past the equipment in the sides of the corridor and found herself in the recovery room.

Her eyes wavered. She could pick out a shadow behind the white sheet that bounded the metal pole and protected the full view of someone on the third bed from where Brianna was.

Brianna could see the figure was moving. Brianna surmised this patient could see her so she took slow measured steps. It was the first time she noticed how loud her steps on the smooth tiled floor was.

Brianna moved aside the sheet and stepped inside. Lying on the bed was a young brunette with dark brown eyes that seemed to peer into Brianna's soul. Those wild eyes, yes, Brianna had eyes like that at some point. The woman laid in bed curled up in a ball. Brianna guessed quickly that she was experiencing the cold shivers that came with withdrawal. Brianna knew she was probably in a bad state right now. But if it continues, she would get worse.

Brianna took a seat next to the bed.

"Are you the nurse that's going to get me better?" the girl asked with a lazy grin.

"I'm going to try. I'm Brianna."

"April. When's the pain going to stop?" she asked as if unwilling to dwell on the introduction.

"Not for a while. When's the last time you took something?"

April's eyes widened as her head rose. "Like, to get a fix?"

"Yes."

"A couple of hours ago," April said lethargically.

Brianna knew that was too soon. That meant she was an advanced user of heroin. April won't last long at this rate. Doing a withdrawal cold turkey on a heroin addict this far gone almost never works. Brianna knew she had to try something more drastic. "Have any left on you?"

April stared blankly at Brianna, unsure.

Brianna rose her palms as if in surrender, "It's okay if you do."

April stared. Her lips opened then closed as it twisted. She turned over on the bed. Her hand reached out, and she pointed her finger. It was in the direction of a bag sitting on a small stool close to the bed. "Yeah, I've got a hit or two left."

"Where?"

"In the front packet."

Brianna walked over to the bag. She opened it up but doesn't reach in. "I'm not going to get pricked with a needle in here am I?"

April shook her head, so that was a no.

Brianna searched the bag and found a container with the drugs.

"I guess you have to throw it away, don't you?" April asked with a wry smile.

"No, we'll put it to good use."

April's mouth was agape, "What do you mean?"

Brianna walked back over to the chair and sat across from her. "There are different ways to help someone in your condition detox. Of course, the ways vary in cost, effectiveness, and risks. The safest way, and cheapest, is to wean you off the drug by giving you the drug until you take less and less of it."

April widened her eyes at that suggestion. "How long will it take?"

Brianna opened the container and looked at the packets. One was in a red-tinted plastic bag; she recognized this one. It was a popular one on the streets, it was not safe because had a lot of additional stuff.

The other packets were the generic versions of the drug these should be safer from her perspective.

"You're gonna be here for the long haul if you really want to change your life and get clean. Minimum, twenty-one days," Brianna said with a wag of her finger.

April just looked on without saying a word.

Brianna continued, "But you won't get any today. I am sure you had enough a couple of hours ago." Brianna closed the container.

April rolled her eyes in response but she still tried to put on a brave smile. She didn't quite know why, but she felt at peace here. It felt like home to her. This was the first time anyone was treating her like a human who existed, and not as a common junkie. She decided at that moment to try and get clean, for Brianna's effort.

CHAPTER 7

A heavy thudding sound shattered Adele's sleep, she jumped awake seeing Brianna in front of the door. The door must have slammed into the wall. Brianna breathed out just once before speaking, "We've gotta go. A call came in saying there's someone bleeding out from several gunshot wounds."

Malvin and Adele popped right out of bed. Brianna rushed out of the room. Malvin and Adele were trailing right behind her. Adele wanted to curse the bad timing but it was not like she was not used to this. Such was the life of Street Nurses she said to herself.

Adele jumped into the back seat. Malvin and Brianna took the front. Malvin started the van up quickly and sped off.

"Where to?"

"Pickinston Road, thirty-seven Pickinston."

Malvin turned off the main road and navigated the smaller district roads. Less likely to catch the attention of cops, they sped down the empty street. Houses passed by like a blur, Adele's tiredness kicked in again. She only got fifteen minutes rest. She was pissed.

"You sure this is a call we should be taking?" Malvin asked. Adele exhaled disgustingly.

What is up with this yellow belly?

Everyone knew this was dangerous. Malvin reminding them was unnecessary in Adele's opinion. If he was going to be a baby about this maybe she should drive.

"Of course. Someone's life is on the line," Brianna replied.

"Yeah, but I mean, can't the real medics take this one?"

"We are real medics."

Adele smiled at the confident retort. Adele knew Brianna was more the picture example of a hero if you could ever find one. Adele had a respect for that still Malvin did have a point. Brianna was sometimes too blinded by her hero philosophy to see the danger.

"I think the pretty boy is trying to say this call sounds dangerous. I mean it does involve gunshots," Adele slyly added.

"You also think we shouldn't respond?" Brianna asked.

"Hell no, these are my favorite," Adele replied. Gangs, especially big ones have a lot of money to spare. Sometimes they would get calls from their shot callers to help patch one of their soldiers up. They paid well notwithstanding the danger.

"What if something happens when we're there?" Malvin asked.

"Let's just focus on the task at hand. Saving this man's life."

Malvin finally surrenders.

The van picks up even more speed as it raced down the empty street. The engine wired and the van skated the departed streets. The lights on it barely provided them clarity looking forward.

It was like they were driving into the abyss. What the darkness held for them was not a worry for Adele. Adele was used to seeing the darkness everywhere. It was a common shade to the light. The light cannot exist without the darkness nor the darkness without the light. The van screeches loudly around a corner, horns blared behind them.

"Sure you didn't kill someone?" Adele joked.

"Pretty sure I didn't," Malvin fired back.

Adele was about to give another retort but the van came to an abrupt stop. No, time, so Adele raced out. "Let's be quick. I'm sure it's only gonna be minutes before the cops arrive," she said as she jogged behind super girl Brianna.

The house was beaten up. The wood on the walls looked rotten from water damage. Window glass was shattered, and there were holes in some places. They all run up the sidewalk towards the house.

Two bodies on the floor, as they step onto the rickety porch, Brianna and Adele gave them a momentary glance, they touched them for a pulse but they were lifeless, there was no trace of life.

"I will look at these guys," the girls turned to Malvin. "Please be safe," Malvin continued. They nodded at him, the two slowed to a more cautious walk inside.

The living room looked like a wild party had been hit by a tornado. Plastic and glass bottles littered the ground. The couch looked brand new even though it had a few stains. The Tv was as wide as the whole side of this wall and looked pretty new as well, except for one big glaring hole on the far right. The rest of the place was a dump, a spread of mold on some wooden furniture and twisting wood in the ceiling.

The smell of cannabis was strong here, Brianna tried to shake off the smell, which was now threatening to choke her. Shattered boards lay carelessly on the floor, Adele took notice of the game station but as Brianna stepped forward, Adele flipped her head to see a young caramel-skinned girl. She appeared just inside the door exiting this living room. She instantly points them to the left.

They moved into view and saw that it was a kitchen. On the ground was a young dark-skinned male slumped on his chest with his bigger friend looking up to see Brianna and Adele.

Brianna and Adele stood beside the young man who they later identified as Kevin. He's still alert. The Big Guy stands up to give them some space. Adele swiftly started unloading the medical bag like clockwork. she laid a small sheet to keep the things she had meticulously laid, sterile. She got out the bandages and the sterile gloves, ripping them, she took out the sleeve and laid it on the sheet for easy retrieval.

"Can you tell me your name?" Brianna asked the young man who was now lying in a pool of his own blood.

"Kevin!" he answered.

"I'm Brianna, and my partner is Adele. We're here to help."

Brianna said to Adele, "Give me gloves, towels, bandages, and the metal forceps. See if you can start an IV."

"Okay," Adele replied as she handed Brianna the medical gloves.

Brianna began to examine the bullet holes. One was just below his shoulder, looked like that was the entry wound. Adele hoped it was not lodged inside. That would be a pain to deal with. Adele removed all the supplies that Brianna asked for. Adele took out the bag. She weaved the line and connected it to the needle, she capped it and slid it perfectly into the bag.

She held it in her left hand, right on the line's end, waiting as she watched Brianna closely.

"Are you having any trouble breathing?" Brianna asked.

"No!" Kevin answered almost screaming as he twitched from time to time.

Brianna counted the bullet holes. "They are three in total," she said looking at Adele. "Two located by the left shoulder blade, and one on the right lower side of his back," she added.

Malvin came out of nowhere and stood at the door entrance.

Brianna looked at him briefly, hopeful.

Malvin shook his head giving her a no.

Brianna nodded and returned her attention to Kevin. "Kevin, we're gonna try and stop the bleeding. We're also going to give you an IV. We might have to take you with us. Okay?"

"Yea," he groaned.

"Can you give me a hand?" Brianna asked Malvin.

"Sure. What do you need?"

"See if you can take care of that lower wound."

Malvin moved to the other side and got on the ground.

Adele fidgeted as she pondered what to do next, she should connect the IV, but how? She needed a vein and unfortunately, he was turned over from the back. His arm was facedown making the vein there, hard to reach. "It's gonna be hard to get him an IV when he's on his stomach."

"Make it work. We can't flip him just yet," Brianna replied.

Brianna and Malvin started applying pressure on the wounds with towels.

"You're doing great, Kevin," Brianna said.

"Is he going to make it?" The bigger man who had been watching asked. Adele figured that if she could get something to keep his arm up, she could insert it.

"I said is he going to make it?" The man asked again. Adele looked up and saw the worry on his face. This was not helping, there was a reason family members stayed outside during surgery. That fear and anxiety was contagious. Adele stood up and pleaded with the big guy to give them room to do their job. He sighed and walked away.

Adele knelt back down and had the IV ready. "Can you hold his arm up till I get this in?" Adele asked Malvin. With one hand, Malvin keeps pressure on the bullet hole on his lower back, and with the other, he lifts Kevin's right arm in the air.

Adele searched for a vein to insert the needle. She found one coursing in the center, Adele heaved a sigh of relief, steadied her hand as she pierced the skin inserting the needle.

She looked around, for a place to rest the IV bag. Nothing, she will need the tack. "Reach in my bag and give me a tack."

Malvin let go of Kevin's arm gingerly and reached into the medical bag, pulled out a thumbtack. He handed her the tack and slammed it into the wall, then she hung the IV Bag on the tack.

She stepped back for a moment to make sure it'll hold. It does. She heaved a sigh of relief. As Adele stoops back down, "Cops are coming!" Adele heard it and wished she did not.

Brianna peeked out the kitchen door, the big guy was gone., "Get the stretcher and start the van!" Brianna screamed.

Adele stood up and ran out of the kitchen. Adele surged out to the front. She jumped over the porch and continued running. She flew around the van and flung it open. She got up on the step and grabbed the stretcher. She flew it out from the slot and the legs opened up hitting the road.

The police sirens were getting closer.

Getting the stretcher up the rocky badly maintained pavement was a struggle. But Adele returned with the stretcher, sweat draining off haphazardly off her skin as if it was battered glass. Brianna and Malvin were almost done with the bandages.

Adele just remembered, she forgot to start the van. Adele shook her head in resolution to deal with that later.

Adele looked around. The place was empty. I guess the girl got the message and bailed as well. Adele tried to steady her breathing as the tiredness crept in. She really needed a nap after this. Hopefully, no one else came to start up another party at this house, two guys outside already were down for the count.

Adele slowed her breathing as the idea stuck in her mind. Not like those two would need any money on them if they were already dead. Yes, she could take their money. They were gangbangers anyways so that money would have better use in her hands.

"I'll be right back. I forgot to start the van," Adele said zooming off before they could ask her questions.

Adele stops as she stood between the two bodies. Looking down at the two bodies, she looked back into the house. Brianna and Malvin seemed focused on Kevin.

Adele knelt down beside the dead bodies and reached into their pocket. She removed their wallets. She opened them up and emptied the contents onto the floor.

The sirens are getting really close now. Multiples of them, flustered, she quickly shoved in the wallets in the men's pockets.

She ran towards the van, jams the key inside and starts it immediately. Those sirens were really loud now. Adele really did not want to go to jail. She had too much life to live and way too many dreams to accomplish. One of them was living well on the outside. She couldn't live well in jail. She rushed out of the van frustrated that they weren't anywhere near the front door. Were they still in the kitchen?

Adele ran inside to rejoin them.

"Let's go! Cops are gonna be here any second!"

Brianna nodded in agreement.

They begin to push the stretcher out of the kitchen. Adele shook the moisture from her hair, always envious of her surroundings. Arms held on tight to the shaking state of the bed, the path to the van was a rough one.

They finally reached. Adele stood at the front as Malvin pushed it in. Adele dropped ungracefully on her bum after shutting the door. Malvin jammed down on the accelerator and rushed down the street, as the first corner came up, he turned sharply. He slowed the van as he moved it onto the next turn.

Malvin looked out the window and looked around as he drove down a more congested street. The sirens flashed suddenly. A crash of red and blue blinded Adele for a second.

Crap, Adele thought, police just drove past them. But they did pass, Adele steadied her breathing as Malvin drove down the road. Two more sirens blared, she could tell because the horns were blaring over the other like a broken record. The cars passed close by and kept on down the road, she hoped.

Finally, the horns were fading. Adele breathed easy as Kevin turned in the bed like a little worm in her hasty assumption. The Iv line shook mightily to his discomfort. The pain will continue for a long while. Adele has never been shot but she could imagine the pain.

"I think we are safe now," Malvin said.

Adele was glad that they were, she was tired and needed rest. She would give the next assignment to supergirl Brianna. Adele got a good amount of money from those two guys on the porch so she should be fine until her next payday.

Yawning, she leaned over Kevin. His eyes opened briefly to ogle her pretty face. She held down the arm that the IV was connected to. "Try to stay still," Adele pointed at the IV line. His eyes followed hers and he nodded weakly. She continued, "It will be alright. We will make you better, ok?"

"Ya," he uttered as sweat rolled off the side of his forehead.

She smiled and tried to make him feel comfortable. She had to do that much at least. Adele wondered what would have happened if they had a run-in with the police. No, such thoughts were not something to consider. Right now, she had to do her best for their current patient.

CHAPTER 8

The more he looked at the scene the more it bored him. He hated responding to calls that had to do with the poor neighborhood, guns, unidentified victims whom to him were usually in the wrong just as much as the perpetrator.

But these were the majority of cases he handled. In his forties, Detective Gray had seen and has had to deal with too much of these cases. There was not much challenge to them, he could wash rinse, repeat.

They always get caught the same way, usually with their pants down.

Gray sighed, leaning off his car, which was parked in front of the house. Detective Gray twiddles his thumbs waiting. Detective Gray was one of the most respected cops in the neighborhood. He knew the trouble makers and gang bangers by name. He was responsible for putting a lot of them behind bars. He fondly reminisced about his glory days when he was always chasing after the bad guys in the street and stared them down, daring them to do their worse. He still got what it takes, but he was becoming bored with chasing street gang members and their constant need to cause trouble.

An officer approaches, placing his gun back into his holster, bringing Detective Gray back to reality. "House is clear. There's no one inside. Two victims on the porch and a lot of blood in the kitchen."

Detective Gray nodded as he stood up straight, he looked around at the other personnel at work. There were at least ten officers on the scene. If the shooters stayed longer it would have been a display of firework. Detective Gray knew it would happen, soon enough.

They won't hide much longer.

Gray also recognized this place. Granted he was not a part of the narcotics unit but he knew some of the more prominent hit spots for gang activity. He was not sure which gang held here but he knew it was a popular safe house for gang members. He had responded to a call here before and it was a shooting. He forgot about most of the specifics. But he knew well enough this was a dangerous place.

Gray wondered if it was like a ritual for gangs to battle each other at certain neutral locations. Best way to avoid hitting innocents.

If that is the case, then I can respect that.

But a crime is a crime, either way, Gray thought. He needed to catch these guys before they start popping off where they are not supposed to.

"Another wonderful shoot-out at the O.K. Corral..." he walks forward, "...a.k.a the Bluff."

The Detective, along with the Officer, walk from the street up to the porch. The Detective looks down at the bodies. "Have we ID'd the bodies yet?"

"No, sir. CSI should be here any second," the officer replied.

The Detective walks into the house. The Officer follows. The place was a mess, Gray tried to avoid stepping on anything noteworthy. Gray knew they could collect prints and DNA off the plastic wrappers and containers. Gray wavered his eyes over the wall. Bullet holes randomly littered them. Considering the only two victims on the scene were on the porch Detective Gray was considering a driveby. This was the quickest way gangs employed to end their foes and also instill fear.

"How many shots would you say came into the house, if you had to guess?" Detective Gray asked.

The officer seemed perturbed but he nodded saying, "Oh, I don't know, sir. Maybe twenty?"

"Sounds about right. Probably at least the same were returned."

"How can you tell?" the Officer asked, shocked.

"These things are never one-sided," Detective Gray replied.

Detective Gray looked out toward the kitchen. "Any idea whose blood that could be?" he asked the officer.

"Maybe one of the men laying outside?"

Detective Gray quickly turned to look at the living room floor. "No blood trail," so that was not possible. He walked to the kitchen to get a closer look.

He looked down at the blood. He could see no trail anywhere from the pool. Unless he flew up through the ceiling, this made no sense. He looked up and noted the kitchen door.

The grill on it, it was still locked from the inside with two golden-colored padlocks. There was no other exit except the door he stood at. Gray pondered the possibilities. Maybe he patched up his wounds and walked out? Still, that would be too quick. Gray looked over on the counters and the shelves. Nothing seemed out of place really, but that might be on purpose. A staged scene perhaps?

Gray scooped out the floor and noticed many footprints the impressions carefully outlined by dirt, were there a lot of people here? He could have been carried out.

"You think we have another victim?" The officer asked.

Gray now shaken out of his thoughts, answered, "Somewhere we do. You said nobody else is in the house?"

"Correct."

"Have a couple of officers patrol in a ten-block radius looking for someone who's losing a lot of blood, or for a body. Couldn't have gone far."

"Yes, sir." The Officer replies, leaving the kitchen.

Detective Gray motioned to the officer, "Tell them to be on guard. It doesn't look like the victim walked out of this house on his own. There's someone with him. Needless to say, that person could be armed and dangerous."

The Officer nodded and walked away.

Detective Gray stayed in the kitchen for a moment longer, looking, from his position, for clues. "Where did you disappear to?"

***

The sun was starting to rise. CSI had just arrived. Their equipment set on the porch. Two CSI male workers were on their knees with their backs hunched over the scene trying to pick out anything that looked out of place.

Detective Gray was on the stair leading up, he watched them. The CSI did not speak. Detective Gray wished they did. He wanted something to go off on, his mind was rolling random pointless thoughts on what really happened here. It was not odd if his first assumption was wrong. No, he should expect to be wrong.

Discerning what happened in a scene can be hard, it was easy to assume the wrong thing with the wrong perspective. Detective Gray was an experienced detective. He had a gritty viewpoint. These CSI never get to experience violence as it happens. That purity allowed them a wider viewpoint.

They were good like that. Still, he wanted to hear something. He wanted to hear what they thought.

"See anything?"

One of the CSI looked up, his eyes had a blankness to it. "Nothing much to see here. Multiple bullet entries, we can assume these two died on the spot."

Detective Gray nodded, "See if they have any identification on them first. That way I can start my investigation while you collect the evidence.

The CSI leaned toward the first man and searched his pockets. Detective Gray stands with a pen and pad in hand, nonchalantly. The CSI finds the first victim's wallet in his back pocket.

"Jarome White."

Detective Gray wrote down the name. The CSI looked down at the patient's head. His brows furrowed, then he looked up at the wallet in his hand.

"Wait a minute."

Detective Gray immediately looked away from the pad. "What?"

The CSI places the ID beside the victim's face, comparing the two. "This isn't him."

"Fake ID?" Detective Gray asked.

The CSI shook his head. "More like the wrong ID."

The Detective crosses out the name on his note pad. "Jarome White is now John Doe."

The CSI placed the wallet on the man's back. He moved to the second victim. He reached into his back pants pocket and pulled out his wallet. He opened the wallet up and looked at the ID.

"ID says, Richard Angler." The CSI said.

Detective Gray was about to write the name but decided against it last minute and asked, "We sure about this one?"

"That isn't him," The CSI answered still staring at the wallet.

"How do you know that you haven't even checked?" Gray bellowed.

The CSI grinned for some reason, then shows the Detective, the second man's ID. "Because this is the first victim's wallet."

For the first time, Detective Gray was intrigued. "How the hell would that happen, each has the other's wallet?" Detective Gray pinched his chin in thought. The CSI got a clear evidence bag out and put a wallet in each.

The CSI looked down at the second victim, he spoke, "Maybe someone else did this?"

Detective Gray rocked his head as he considered that. There would be no reason for them to have each other's wallets. But why would someone switch the wallets? It was not like it could trick anybody. Someone would look at the faces and know. It made no sense.

It had to be an accident or…

Detective Gray widened his eyes. "Is there any money inside?" The CSI froze. He looked up with a pensive face and must have realized what Detective Gray was getting at. The CSI checked the wallets and confirmed Detective Gray's thought.

"No, no money inside," the CSI uttered.

Gray shook his head. "So, we have a thief too."

The second CSI peered through the door and said as he looked at Gray. "A lot of people were here last night I reckon. Someone must have seen it as an opportunity to rob these two."

The first CSI spat out, "Damn."

Detective Gray had seen it all, this wasn't new to him. He just did not expect to see it here. People would be kicking to get out of here as fast as possible. Detective Gray tilted his jaw as he took one last look at the kitchen.

Though, it was a drive-by, if the gang left as quickly as expected. These two men would be ripe for the picking. It would not be hard to hide out the initial shooting. When the place had become deserted, the culprit came to pick their pockets.

If there were a lot of people in this place, it will be hard to find that person. Detective Gray had to take note of this but he won't be particularly driven to find that person unless it was the person who left the blood on the floor inside. Or at least whoever carried him out, someone must have carried him out, he left no blood trail.

Detective Gray sighed, "Check the wallets for traces of blood along with the usual when you are done."

The CSI nodded and returned the wallets to the bags. Detective Gray's radio blipped as the noise boomed, he grabbed it.

"Detective Gray here," he said into the mouthpiece.

The noise rumbled briefly before it clicked and a voice spoke, "Sir we found an abandoned car. We got some gunshot holes on it."

The getaway car? It must be my lucky day.

"Alright cordon off the area. I will be down there now," Detective Gray replied as he slid the radio onto his belt. "I am going. Call me if you find anything,"

The two CSI's nodded their head in response. Detective Gray walked away and made his way to the car. Shutting the door, he leaned back into the chair and exhaled softly, suffice to say he was in no hurry to go down there. He wondered who he would catch first, the victim or the perpetrator?

Hmm, maybe I should say which perpetrator?

It was still likely that the person whose blood splattered all over the kitchen is a thief. Well if he finds that person, he would hang the crime over their head and got them to spill info on what really happened last night.

He started the car, revving it to life. He drew himself off the sidewalk and into the heavy morning traffic that loomed ahead.

Grabbing his jacket and pushing aside the sides of the open front he stepped out onto the sidewalk. He looked around, the media was there, a bit too much he thought. He knew they risked making it a public case if they called it a drive-by. He hated the media. They were like vultures and stroked the iron hot when they could. Hot news sells, they will be an annoyance until another interesting news comes along. Hopefully, a politician does something stupid that was a sure way to make them lose interest in this case.

Other than them, a few people standing looked on with curiosity. The usual gossip would start. Detective Gray wished he could ask them himself but he knew that people in this community were distrustful of police.

He would get nowhere bothering to seek eyewitnesses. He moved off into the direction of the others. They stood in front of an alleyway, two officers kept them at bay and tried to push them back. As He passed, one reporter sees him and tried to maneuver to stop him. He sped up, slipping in behind one of the officers and before the reporter could meet up, another officer stopped him.

The alleyway was smashed between a derelict apartment building and a business complex. The air in that path was stuffy, and there was water streaming in the center. Detective Gray figured it was sewage water from one of the buildings. A silver car was haphazardly parked with one wheel on the elevated ramp.

There was one CSI from what Detective Gray could see, at least five officers yawning and watching out for anything. He watched the CSI photographing the abandoned vehicle.

Detective Gray motions one of the officers, "Find out if they got anything new from the house, oh ask them if they found that missing victim as well."

The officer nodded and headed out as instructed. Gray stands over the car. He took out a pad and writes down something. No key left in the ignition, no signs that they crashed.

"You found anything inside the glove compartment?" Gray asked.

The CSI shook his head. "We got a hit on the license plate at least." Another officer chimed in.

Good, we can follow that lead as well.

There were visible bloodstains on the floorboard and seats. Bullets in the window and door frame of the car, Gray mused to himself the possibility that there might be more than one victim now.

We should check the hospitals.

"Any recent new patients in the hospital with gunshot injuries?" Grays asks no one in particular.

The officer shook his head. "They told us no last time we checked."

"Check again, one of these persons could check-in at any time," Gray replied.

"The staff said they will alert us if anyone comes in."

"Good."

A police officer approaches the detective.

"Any update on the search for the missing victim from the house?" Gray asks.

"No, sir. We searched the ten blocks radius and it was all clear. Not even a drop of blood," he said.

"Okay. Well, have your men regroup and go on a ten-block search from this location. There appears to be a blood trail here. Maybe we'll get lucky with this one."

"We'll get started right away. The reporters want to know if you are ready to make a statement."

Detective Gray sighed, "When I'm done here, I'll make sure to say hello."

"Okay. I'll let them know."

The Police Officer walked away and toward the main street.

CHAPTER 9

Brianna shook suddenly. Her eyes peeled open to see Mary Jane walked over to Brianna and Malvin, her footsteps woke them up.

Brianna was tired. So was Malvin, he was rocking his head drowsily opposite her on the bench. In the waiting room, across from where they sat in the makeshift Operating Room.

The quietness kept her calm. As much as she was tired, she couldn't sleep on the bed until she was sure Kelvin was ok.

Mary Jane came out, her light blue gown with patterned dots layered over the shade. Her scrubs have been designed with bloodstains.

The Doctor knelt down, removing her face mask.

"How is he?" Brianna asked almost coughing.

"Lucky. Still hanging in there," Mary Jane replied.

Brianna let out a sigh of relief. Malvin smiles, putting his hand on Brianna's knee. They smile at each other for a moment.

Mary Jane continued, "He'll need a lot of rest and monitoring. The two wounds in his shoulder blade had exit points. The one in his lower back did not, but I was able to find the bullet and remove it."

"Thank you so much."

Mary Jane grinned and shrugged. "No problem."

"Angelic is with him now. I think you should go rest, there's nothing you can do for him right now. In the morning you can say hello." Brianna and Malvin both stood. They each shook Mary Jane's hand.

Brianna and Malvin leave to go get some rest. They entered the room and found Adele already fast asleep. Brianna walked \cautiously to avoid waking her.

Brianna turned towards Malvin. He looked like he was about to fall over from fatigue. She really did put a lot of pressure on her team. But she admired that about them. They never turned their backs on her no matter how many dangerous situations she dragged them into. This was a dangerous one. But they came with her and stuck with her without complaint. Especially, Malvin, she did tell him to get a nap. But he stayed with her, he must be itching to get some proper sleep. Brianna smiled to herself, her back was starting to ache as well.

This job would make her older than her past addiction ever would. "Nice work tonight."

Malvin nodded. "Thanks." Malvin looked away as he walked past her. Brianna pondered it, she realized something was wrong. She had known Malvin long enough to know when something was bothering her. His mood was a bit more contemplative; it was like he was lost.

"What's wrong?" she asked.

"Nothing," Malvin muttered without looking at her.

"We've known each other since we were kids, I know when there's something on your mind. What is it?" Brianna asked, peeking a look at Adele's motionless frame.

Malvin sits down on his bed, pensive for words. Brianna sat down on her bed from across him.

"I know we helped save a boy's life tonight, but I think we should stop doing those sorts of calls," he finally said reluctantly.

"What?" Brianna asked, surprised by what he said.

Malvin breathed out and faced her. "For one, he would have probably died if we couldn't have gotten a hold of Mary Jane. We're only nurses. Not doctors, or the way I think you see it, superheroes."

She frowned, rocking back and forth. "You know that's not how I see myself. I'm just trying to help people."

"But at what cost? Whoever shot at those people, they could have come back to finish the job. They could have started shooting again. I'm all for saving people and helping those less fortunate, but I'm not going to risk my life, and watch you risk yours, over dangerous people."

Brianna was not expecting this. Brianna was not and had never been ignorant about the fact that she often dragged them into dangerous situations. She never denied that. She breathed out as she twiddled her fingers in thought. It was bad enough shouldering that burden. Brianna was not going to stop helping people. If Brianna started picking and choosing how to help, she would be no different from hospitals.

She already promised herself long to not become political like them. The Street nurses were a saving grace to this society. It provided something that no one else could. Plus, if it did not exist, if her mother did not create it the way that it is now, Brianna would not have been saved.

"You can't be serious," Brianna said, she was not asking. She could tell he was serious. But she was trying to belay his motivation even if it was just a tilt in her direction. Malvin had made these complaints before. But each time she shot him down he got more determined with each complaint.

Brianna groaned inwardly. Malvin might leave if she does not navigate this discussion wisely.

"I wouldn't say it if I wasn't," he answered.

"We do this..." she licked her lips. "I do this for the people that society has turned their backs on. A person like Kevin needs to know someone is looking out for him in his most dire time. We can give people a second chance."

"What about yours. What if something happens to you when you're on one of these dangerous calls. It's not like we can wait for the police," he retorted.

"This is my second chance. Everything now is just a bonus."

Malvin laid down. Looking up at the ceiling, he said nothing. Was he done? Brianna hoped he was. She really did not want to lose his support. Brianna kept staring at him from where she sat.

"It won't last forever and I don't want to be there when it ends." Malvin turns to his side, facing away from Brianna. "Goodnight, Brianna."

Brianna sat on her bed staring at his now sleeping frame. She sighed and kicked herself for being so stubborn. It was not like he was wrong. She pondered what was worse, what she was now or what she feared she would become. But Brianna knew she could not live with herself any other way. Would it end? They had a sponsor but she wasn't sure for how long.

Without money, this operation would not be possible. They had a few different sponsors before this one. From what Angelic has told her, they always start out so kind and offhanded. But the more money they sank into the operation, the more control they wanted. Angelic joked that they always cut ties with a sponsor after a year. This current sponsor was through Mary Jane and he had been supporting them for a little over a year.

Brianna wondered when this sponsor would start chipping away at their philosophies and beliefs? They might never find another sponsor if they cut this one off for some reason. A day might come when they would have to accept whatever the sponsors needed. Brianna tried to take everything in.

But she resolved to just do her best and see what the world has in store for her. "Goodnight, Malvin."

CHAPTER 10

Brianna drew in puffs from the butt trying to numb the doubt in her mind. Malvin was still sleeping and that made her glad. She was not sure if she could say anything to him after last night. He was still around so she could not complain. But that discussion really put her on the spot and got her thinking. Brianna hated to think too much about how easily destructible Street Nurses was as an organization.

She knew Street Nurses, this thing her and Angelic created was always on the edge of dying. The morning sun had fully risen. Brianna sat on the steps smoking a cigarette trying not to think about the things that worried her.

She groaned because she really could not get it out of mind now.

Was I really considering this? I should not even bother.

Still, Brianna needed to find a way to keep Street Nurses going. Yes, it was hard and equally dangerous work but she had to reach a compromise. At least that, Brianna thought.

But what?

"You know those things will kill you."

Brianna turned to see Mary Jane's scrutinizing smirk staring at her while Adele hovered behind her. She suddenly had a flashback of how she had met Mary Jane. Angelic had introduced them shortly after she decided to get clean. Mary Jane took her under her wings and mentored her like a mother would. She was more than just a middleman between the street nurses and their sponsors, and now Brianna was afraid she might lose all this; the family bond, the help they rendered.

Mary Jane continued, snapping her right back to the present. "If you need anything or if there's any change in Kevin's condition, you know to call me."

They used up a good amount of supplies for the last set of emergencies they had. Brianna needed to ask about that. "What about supplies?"

"You'll have them by the end of the week. Our sponsor says he might have a surprise for you," Mary Jane answered.

"A surprise? Like what?"

"Didn't say, only that it would be very useful for your operation."

Brianna looks at Adele, who shrugs.

"I'll see you guys soon."

Mary Jane climbed up the steps to her car parked on the street.

Brianna turned to Adele who was still moving past her, "You headed out?"

"Yeah, for a little while. Got some things I gotta do." Adele's smile widened, "Shouldn't you get some rest. You can't save the world if you fall asleep."

"Yeah, I'm going there now."

Adele nodded as she walked away.

Brianna took one last drag from her cigarette before putting it out. She stood up about to head inside when she heard someone call out very faintly.

She turns and sees a man with caramel skin calling out to her while clutching his legs. "Help." His pants were covered in blood.

Brianna swiftly jumped into action, running down the steps to the man's side. She drapes his arm around her and helps him into the building.

When she reached under the building and starts to get tired. She calls out to Malvin for help but there was no reply even after she yelled his name. Maybe he was still asleep she thought to herself. Brianna looked around and wished there was a bed to lay this guy in so carrying him would be easier.

"Help, Malvin! Help!" she called out again.

They should probably get a panic button in case of emergencies like this. Brianna thought as she laid the man down on the ground, she almost went with him. He breathed heavy; his eyes rolled wearily to the pain he was in. Brianna had to get him help. What was she going to do now? Best to run upstairs and wake him up, she turned towards the injured man and pleads with him.

"Hey, calm down, you are going to be okay. Alright?"

The injured man nodded to her words while still gritting his teeth in pain.

"I am Brianna, I am a street nurse and I help people like you. Would you mind telling me who you are and how you got hurt?" she asked the man who looked   calmer.
"Uhmm, my name is Dillion, I got shot by…ahh this hurts so bad" The man whom she had come to know as Dillion screamed.

"Listen, Dillion, it's okay, I am here now, and my team and I will…" she is interrupted by thundering steps. She turned around and saw Malvin running down the steps stopping briefly to scope out what was before him.

"Help me get him downstairs," She pleaded before he even got close.

Malvin walked over to the other side and together they begin to take him to the basement. From there they carried him to a bed in the ward.

They laid him on a bed. Brianna instructed Malvin to cut the pants. She turns outside. She raced outside and came back with a trolley. Malvin already sliced one side of the pants and drew it off from the other side. Throwing it onto a roll of paper on the side, the man groaned as he tried lifting himself up off the bed.

Malvin grabs the man's right shoulder and eased down slowly. "Please we know it hurts but you have to stay still, ok?"

He gave Malvin a brisk nod before leaning back. Malvin did a blood test with the meter. "I will go get the blood bag," He said as he rushed off hurriedly.

Brianna nodded as she looked over at the leg. There was a blue handkerchief tied around it, just under the knee. There was a thin white cloth soaked red over the lower part of his leg just barely over the ankle. Brianna slip-on gloves and carefully untied and unwrapped the right leg. She revealed two holes.

She almost assumed a stab wound but corrected her assumption as she noted how small and circular, they were. The blood spewing forth made her believe it was a gunshot wound.

Brianna knew this was going to be difficult. She used water and her gloved hands to wash off the blood caked on his leg. From there she swiftly reached for a thick gauze pad and pressed hard on the first entry wound.

Brianna looked up to see the man watching with heavy breathing. She wondered how he must be feeling right now watching himself bleed out. But he kept himself calm throughout. She concluded that he probably had seen a lot in his life and that frightened her. But she needed his help right now since Malvin was not here. "Could you hold this?" Brianna asked.

The man nodded and grabbed hold of the pad. She slid his hands closer to the edge while she grabbed the micropore tape and pasted a number of strips quickly onto the center of the pad. She then grabbed the crepe bandage and proceeded to wrap that around that large section of his leg.

By the time she was done, Malvin arrived with the blood and hooked it to him. Malvin helped her with the second wound as she wrapped that as well. After she was done, she checked the bandages for any sign of leakage. She hoped to God he did not have any internal bleeding. It was very likely with a leg injury such as this since the leg had very close arteries and veins that pretty much would be his death if the bullet nicked them.

Brianna might have to call Mary Jane and tell her about this new patient just in case his condition gets worse. The injured man laid on a bed. His leg had been neatly bandaged. He flexed his face as he fidgeted on the bed to get a comfortable enough position. He breathed out as he slid back more lazily.

He seemed to be at ease even with a tense face like that. Even though he was feeling pain at least he was comfortable. Still, Brianna wanted to know what happened to him just in case she missed something. She might be wrong about the whole bullet thing.

"You don't have to answer if you don't want to, but how did this happen?" Brianna asks.

The injured man doesn't say anything.

Brianna decided to let it go. He was probably a criminal and did not want to talk, lest he admits to a crime. She understood that much about this kind of people. She turned around to throw her gloves into the red biohazard bags.

"Who's that in the room beside me?" The injured man asked. Brianna was shocked to hear his voice and she was more concerned that he was asking about Kevin.

"We can't tell you that," Malvin answered back.

"No, you can tell me, and you will," the injured man retorted.

Brianna turned back around. "Why's that?"

The injured man looked Brianna square in the eyes. "Because if that's who I think it is, you're gonna have a serious problem on your hands."

"Hey! We saved your life. You could have bled out. Now you're threatening us?" Malvin fired back at him.

The injured man smiled, "Thank you. I appreciate it. For saving my life. Not his."

Brianna and Malvin exchanged glances, surprised at the man's sudden demeanor.

Brianna flexed her jaw and her arm to hide the fear she was battling with, unsure of how to respond. She tries to stay calm. This was the first time this has happened. She was used to gang members and criminals coming in for help.

Most of them knew about their organization, a secret that was well protected in the inner community. They were too poor or too 'hot' to go to the hospital. Normally the only place for them was the grave and society couldn't be bothered.

Brianna did not think that was fine. She would help them. Now her help seems pointless before the truth, blood runs deep. In the streets, the hatred between gangs runs deeper than that. It was unlikely she would be able to talk him out of doing anything to Kelvin.

Brianna turned to Malvin, "Can you stay here with him while I step out for a moment?"

"Of course," Malvin said.

"I'll be right back," Brianna said to both of them. The injured man said nothing as he just watched Brianna leave.

Brianna finally breathed out. She was feeling burnt. She almost could say she was losing herself to this job. Brianna was not sure what she should do. He was serious. Brianna could not let Kelvin leave; he was still recovering.

Upstairs was a bit far from where they kept their equipment. They could carry some essentials to the room they used.

Upstairs was where they slept. It would be a security threat to them. Brianna did not know Kelvin. But Brianna would feel worse if that man harmed Kelvin. It was better this way.

Brianna walked up to Angelic who's at her post.

"You alright?" Angelic smiled up at Brianna.

"We have a problem."

"What is it?"

"First thing, can we move Kevin upstairs?"

"But those are just empty apartments," Angelic replied throwing her a suspicious look.

"I know."

"I guess it's doable, as long as he stays within eyes shot so we can monitor him," she shrugs.

"Okay. Good." Brianna stood there wondering if she should tell Angelic. Was he serious? He could just be bluffing, Brianna thought.

I hate this. Malvin was right…but I have to deal with it.

Angelic rocked her to the side. Angelic's eyes became more potent. "Is that it?"

"We're gonna need some help," Brianna replied.

Angelic reached for the phone, Brianna looked like she was about to speak. Angelic froze. "You need me to call Mary Jane back in?" Angelic asks.

"No, I was thinking, help from someone a little more muscular, tougher."

Angelic leaned back, her eyes widened. Her hand sunk back, a flutter of eyes, sad and deeply probing at Brianna's eyes. Angelic's body language was now tense like Brianna's.

"Wait, what are we talking about here…" Her eyes widened. She shook her head rapidly as if shaking off the torpor off. "That man you brought in…"

"Yes, him."

"So, what the two of them got into an argument or something?"

Brianna respected Angelic's innocence but she needed to honest about the situation as it was right now. "He knows Kelvin. I think they were on opposing sides of the shooting that caused their injuries."

"Is there any way to talk to hi…"

Brianna interrupted her by shaking her head before she could finish.

"I don't see any possibility of talking him out of his anger," Brianna replied.

Angelic shook her head. Her hand slid up the top side of hair pushing it to the side as she sighed, "I don't know what to say. I don't know anyone myself."

"Well, we need someone. Where can we find someone right now?"

Angelic shrugged. "I couldn't tell you. Besides we can't just call anyone."

"Ya, I know. We need to vet them. We have put too much into this place to have just anyone ruin it. I just..."

Angelic laid her palm out. "Don't be stressed. I am sure we can figure it out later but for right now there is not much we can do."

Brianna snorted. "I am an idiot. Should have seen this coming. This man seriously wants to…to, to kill Kelvin. I don't know what else to do."

Angelic stood up and grabbed Brianna's shoulder. "Don't worry it will be ok. We will figure it out. I will make some calls and see if I can find someone." She smiled at Brianna, "Come on you are usually more optimistic than this."

Brianna leaned forward with her hands firmly rooted on the desk. "I still am but that might be the problem. We have been taking these types of calls and we never not once considered this would happen."

Angelic opened her lips to talk, but she closed them. She patted Brianna on the shoulder. Angelic looked to the side before she said, "Don't be hard on yourself because of that. It is hard to get help nowadays. Not everyone sees things our way."

Most people did not see how I think.

Brianna straightened. "Let us move Kelvin upstairs."

Brianna arrived back into the ward with Angelic. Brianna called out Malvin.

Brianna "How is he?" she asked.

"He asked me how soon he will be able to walk," Malvin replied cupping his face in his palm.

That sent chills down Brianna's spine. He was already thinking of what he wanted to do when he recovered. He was pretty much itching to leave, Brianna feared. Brianna spoke, "We are moving Kelvin. Let us do this quietly."

The two of them nodded and all made their way to the room where Kelvin was.

Kelvin looked up with droopy eyes. "Hey."

"We are moving you," Brianna said.

Kelvin fidgeted. "Is that guy…"

Brianna looked away when she said, "Let us not talk about him."

Kelvin labored himself into a sitting position, Angelic rushed to his side. "He wants to kill me can't you see?"

Brianna did not want to answer him. Malvin answered, "He might want to harm you but he can't because his leg is seriously injured.

"His leg can heal."

Malvin could not retort to that. Brianna nodded and said, "Hold on Kelvin we will take you upstairs. Trust me you will be fine until you heal."

Malvin wanted so bad to ask him what he had done to Dillion to make him want to hurt him despite being hurt himself, but he decided against it last minute.

Kelvin nodded. Brianna and Malvin carted the bed through the halls and made their way into the lift. From there they put him in one of the rooms.

He went to sleep almost immediately. Brianna reasoned he was still tired. He deserved the rest. She just hoped they could keep him safe.

On the way back from his room, Malvin and Brianna said nothing, Malvin had every right to gloat about being right, but he didn't, and Brianna appreciated that. Brianna felt like saying one thing.

"Thank you."

Malvin turned towards Brianna with an odd look before it softened. He nodded and left to get some sleep.

Angelic walked to Brianna. "You ok?"

"I'm ok, we have to be vigilant, we all have to do what we can." She replied her eyes still trailing after Malvin.

CHAPTER 11

Adele walked briskly. The cold atmosphere kept her sheltered and calm. She was still tired. Adele would cry her pain from her lethargic bones and it would still make little difference to her. Avoiding the fleeting bodies that passed around so effortlessly, she was on auto. But her resolve kept weaving through all the struggles in her life. Whether it be other people in this dirty musty street or the deadly job of always having to narrowly avoid gunshots and police. Adele resolved to sleep at her house more. Every time she slept at work; she was woken up every five minutes.

This might be me reaching. Though hearing that argument between Brianna and Malvin was interesting it was also a dead-end for Malvin. No way Brianna would listen to him, we all knew that.

Still, the Street Nurses were quite famous, or is it infamous? It was an annoying fact that did make her slightly happy. Adele got more work. She was happy with that fact but she had to accept that more work meant less sleep. Adele was determined to see this through.

She crossed the street and walked into a large Bank. Inside, a stiffer cold grip as the clean room leaves her nose feeling an ease that tickled her skin. There were not many people on the queue. But only two tellers, this will take a while either way.

She heaved out of frustration. Walking actually helped to shake off the sleepiness. Standing still will do her a nice solid right now, Adele almost laughed at the possibility of falling over in the line because she was tired.

Hilarious…

Adele believed in the basic concept of working hard, for now, to have an endless vacation later. That was what she had been aiming for since she lost her job and standing in the legit medical industry.

She worked hard in that industry, she worked long hours and spent much of her sweat and for what? She was kicked out and spat out with a blacklist on her name everywhere she went. Her license was revoked, her old friends turned their backs on her. Actually, they became witnesses against her. This was one of her biggest motivations for taking the street nurses job when she was offered it by Angelic.

She was at an all-time low back then. She felt like there was no hope for her. But here she was, finding new life as a Street Nurse. Adele like Brianna got a second chance so Adele understood how Brianna felt. Finding purpose is difficult, Adele did not really have a purpose. She just wanted to make as much money as possible. Because she believed the Street Nurses was temporary.

Adele had to lean on this exit strategy. Adele envied Brianna and her strict goal chasing, Adele was just not like that. Adele only wanted to get her payday and move on to the next one.

A teller calls out to the next person in line. It's Adele. She walks over to the teller.

"Hello. How are you today?" The teller asked.

"Very good," Adele replied.

"Great, what can I do for you today?"

"I'd like to make a deposit into my account."

"No problem."

Adele slid the Teller a deposit slip alongside a wad of cash. This was the same cash she took from the dead victims. Adele did not care about the morals of it. She had to do what she could to get where she needed to go. In this life, the powerful played the game the way they did because they could break the less powerful like her. Adele needed as much insurance just in case that happens.

The Teller entered some information into her computer and then scanned the deposit slip.

Teller asked, "Would you like a receipt?"

"Yes, please."

The women exchange a friendly smile with each other. The Teller printed out a receipt and handed it to Adele.

"Will that be everything?"

Adele wished she could tell her she had more money to deposit. Adele was only starting, soon she would try and expand into other territories. Who knows what was in store for her as long as she saved wisely? "That's it, for today."

"You have a wonderful day."

"You too." She responded with a wide smile.

Adele walked away from the counter with a jump in her step. Adele walked past the security who nodded in acknowledgment, she returned his nod as she stepped into the warm jungle of the city.

Now she wanted to quench her thirst. The insatiable thirst that all humans had, Adele looked up and smiled as the soft wind caressed her frame. She smiled and decided she would get a drink to celebrate her accomplishment.

She went around the corner, her feet pounding the ground. She navigated her way to the place, *Harry's Pub*. They had a good selection. She stepped in, the air inside the pub was warm. It was not unbearable as it had a light aftertaste of Irish moss mixed with the strong scent of beer, Adele could fall asleep with the aroma. She was used to the smell of being born into a working family. A father who worked really hard and drank occasionally. He was quite fine. Adele flexed her face in a deep frown.

I need to stop thinking of my father.

Adele studied her environment briefly, there was only one person. The tables were smooth light brown wood, padded wooden chairs. A few pictures of rock bands on the walls, the chandelier was still broken Adele considered. She took a barstool beside an Asian man. He mouthed a hello towards her. She nodded at him. He averted his gaze. But Adele had to admit he looked quite out of place here, he looked like a college student.

But the big mug he was downing surprised her. Adele relaxed as he finished the drink and left. Adele waved at the bartender. "What do you need?" the jolly-looking bartender asks her.

"Quart of Beer,"

He shook his head affirmatively and went to get her order. He returned with it a minute later and she began sipping eagerly. Enjoying the beer by herself, she saw the press conference, the news was carrying it. Under the speaking man standing at the podium was *Missing Person from suspected Gang Shooting*.

Was this man talking about the shooting they had responded to a couple of days ago? They had to make sure they did not leave anything at the scene that could be traced back to them. Though it was a close call and it was likely they did leave more evidence than they might not have thought about.

"Can you turn that up?" Adele asked.

The bartender obliged her and turned up the TV's volume.

The man continued, "Right now, we don't have that much information other than there was a shooting that took place in the early hours of the morning. We have two deceased and one missing person. We believe this missing person, is severely injured and in need of emergency medical treatment. The said person has not been identified by the Police yet but will give you it shortly when it becomes available. The Police have cause to believe that he did not leave the crime scene on his own."

Adele frowned. The police were smarter than she thought.

Damn, how did they figure out that much? She has to tell Brianna about this.

"If you have helped this man, or know where he is, please contact the Atlanta Police Department, immediately. There is a money reward for information leading to this man's whereabouts."

Adele's eyes widen.

A reporter stepped forward to ask a question. "Can you tell us anything about the vehicle you've been searching in the ally some distance from the shooting scene, and if it's connected to the shooting."

"At this time, we believe it is linked to the shooting, and the people or person who dumped it might have been wounded. Other than that, there's nothing I can share with you and the public about this ongoing investigation."

Adele turned her attention away from the TV. She took one last long sip from her beer. Kelvin would soon be released. Once he is, if he is just picked up by police it wouldn't be their responsibility.

Adele knew he won't say something. The community knew fully well that they should keep the place a secret to protect it for other people from the inner community.

If he does, Adele got her reward money already so that should be fine. She was considering tipping off the Police for the ransom promised. Yes, Adele could pass him on to the police, after all, he was a criminal. Actually, she was doing the community a service getting him off the street. It was a good business.

They pay Street Nurses for patching them up, and then they call the police to pick them up. Collect the reward money, they would be making a killing.

Oh, wait, no I would be making a killing.

She dropped a couple of dollars on the bar. She heads for the exit, now with an even bigger jump in her step.

CHAPTER 12

Brianna was under the underpass. She and Adele were helping some homeless people as usual. Brianna could not deny that Adele was more energetic than usual. Guess she went home to get some well-needed sleep. Brianna began to wonder how long it had been since she went home. It had been months.

Brianna waved old appliances as she approaches a woman. The woman was standing before a big box, batches of clothes were all around her. Her hair was badly stringed out and gray even with her rather young but rough face. She hands the homeless woman a couple of unused syringes.

"How are you?" Brianna asked.

"Oh, you know. Things are never great when your home is under a bridge."

Brianna nodded with a knowing smile. "Well, it's never too early to turn your life around."

"I know. I know."

The Homeless Woman turned around and headed back over to her living area.

"Anyone else needs fresh needles?"

A couple of other homeless people made their way over to Brianna. She handed them the remaining needles accordingly. Brianna joined Adele by their van, adjacent from the bridge they were just at.

"How is passing out needles helping these people?" Adele asked.

"They're going to use whether they have new or used needles. Give them fresh ones and we can help curb some of the diseases out here on these streets."

Adele rocked her head to the side. "You don't feel like we're just encouraging these people to use?"

"If I did, I wouldn't be passing these out. You feel that way?"

"I think we - well, not we, but you know what I mean..."

Brianna nodded yes.

"... should be doing everything we can to make it difficult for them to find needles. Drugs. Whatever. Then maybe they'd stop using."

"Or they'd go to more extreme lengths to get their drugs."

Adele shrugs twirled, Brianna and Adele got into the van. The warmness of the van threw off the cold that bit at their skin.

"We could go back and forth on this one all day," Adele continued as she started the van.

"Luckily for you, we don't have time."

"For me?" Adele laughed shaking her head. "I think I'd get you to start seeing it my way."

Brianna waved her off. "Ha. Never. You know I can be thick-headed."

"Now there's something we can agree on."

They both giggled. This back and forth was all in good fun, Brianna appreciated Adele's voice. She kept Brianna on the ground. Adele was a more practical nurse, and she is good at what she does. She was swift and pretty good at innovating her way out of any problem. She had more experience with accidents and emergencies than Malvin.

They drove off and tried to make their way back. Close to their location, the Van sat at a red light. Adele rolled her eyes, then suddenly asked, "You think Melvin is really going to be able to find someone to help us beef up security?"

"Sure. Why not? It can't be that hard," Brianna answered turning to look at her.

"You should have sent me. I'm way tougher than, Mel."

Brianna did not deny that. Adele had a calmness in the face of danger that Brianna often respected. To say she was a badass was an understatement, Brianna thought. "He's got good people skills. He's friendly. You'd just scare everyone away."

"I'm not that bad - most of the time. Some people are jerks and need to be told off sometimes," she answered nudging Brianna playfully.

Brianna answered. "If he can't, I guess we'll post a help wanted ad."

Adele motioned her hands like she was holding a paper quite pompously Brianna noted. "Attention. Looking for someone that can defend him/herself and protect others. Keep secrets. At times break the law. Also, work in a secret hospital." Adele said pretending to read the ad.

Brianna smiled, "Sounds exciting to me."

Looking out the windshield of the van they both saw a man about to cross the street. As he stepped off the curb, he suddenly collapsed.

The light turns green.

Brianna opened her lips and slowly spoke, "Go over to..."

"I saw him," Adele replied before she could complete her request. With her eyebrows twisted down and her jaw tight, Adele took the van over to the curb. Brianna jumped out to help the man.

Brianna stretched her hand to the man who took it. She pulled him back to his feet.

He was scruffy looking even though he wore a suit.

"Thanks," he said as he got on his feet.

"You okay?" Brianna asked.

"I think so."

He tried to put weight on it. He had a grimace on his face.

"You need me to look at it?" Brianna asked.

"Why? Who are you?" the man asked, shocked.

"I'm Brianna. You can call me, Bri. I'm a nurse."

"Nice to meet you, Bri. No need. I'm fine. Just gotta walk it off."

Brianna knew he was not fine. "You sure?"

"Positive," The man replied, desperate to end the conversation.

Brianna agreed reluctantly. "Okay. Well, you have a good day, sir."

"Don't call me sir. You're making me feel old." He joked, trying to smile through his obvious pain. He suddenly stopped as he is about to leave. "I'm Aaron."

Brianna tilts her head, "It was nice to meet you, Aaron. You take care of yourself. Be more careful next time."

Aaron does his best to walk away. Brianna watched him for a moment before getting back into the van.

They drove away. Brianna looked out the side of the window as they rounded the corner as she watched his figure fade.

"He was acting tough," Adele said to Brianna.

"I know. But if he does not want our help, I can't do much."

"I hope he can walk with that…" Adele replied.

Brianna breathed out. The one thing she could not do was going against someone's wishes. It was one of the most important rules medical practitioners had to respect and keep. Brianna was very good at obeying the law but she did respect the ethics of medicine and always upholds them.

They soon got back. April laid on her bed curled up in a ball, sweating enough to make the covers wet.

Brianna was worried and concerned. "How you holding up?" she asks looking over her.

April shivered as she stretched out her arms. "Barely. I don't know how much longer I can take this," she answered still shivering and sweating.

"How much do you usually take when you were fully using?"

"Twenty milligrams. Each time."

"Okay. Let's not do the full dosage as usual." Brianna replied.

"So, I can?"

Brianna shook her head in affirmation. April grabbed her bag to get her drugs. Brianna walked towards the door and stopped halfway through the door.

"I'll send in Angelic to watch you while you do it."

April froze instantly, then her eyes opened wider as she leaned to the right. "You're not gonna be with me?"

"I can't," Brianna said.

"Why?"

Brianna looked at April knowing she probably felt judged and maybe was even losing trust in her. But Brianna was not going to aggravate her own past problems.

"Just can't be here when you do it. I'll be with you every step of the way, but I cannot be there when you are using. I'll check back with you in a little while."

Brianna walked away from the room arriving at Angelic's post. "Can you go to April's room and keep an eye on her while she uses."

"Of course." Angelic said, getting out of her chair and headed towards April's room.

"Stop, man! Stop!" Brianna heard someone scream.

Was that Kelvin?

Brianna turned her head jerked up and a surge of fear rushed through her. Her feet were on auto, she rushed down the hall. As Brianna ran, she's joined by Adele who's racing to Kelvin's room as well.

"What's going on?!" Adele exclaimed. Brianna's mind raced with the many possibilities of what could be happening. Brianna had no time to curse herself right now, much less guess Kelvin's fate.

The scream intensified as they approached his room. Brianna pushed open Kelvin's door to see the injured man standing over Kelvin, pulling at his stitches.

"What the hell are you doing?" Brianna screamed, in shock. Brianna and Adele did not hesitate neither did the gangster as he continued to hurt Kelvin. They jumped on the gangster, trying to pull him away from Kelvin.

The gangster had got a few of the bullet holes reopened and there was blood everywhere. Kelvin winced in pain as the gangster was being dragged away. The gangster hits Adele hard with his elbow as she had her hands wrapped around his neck. Adele falls to the ground and grunts in pain.

He then moved away from the bed and focused on Brianna, kicking her in the leg. Brianna winces as her leg seized up in pain. Adele recovered quickly and jumped on his back again, wrapping her arms around his neck harder.

"Get off of me!" the gangster yells. Brianna reached after him, but he swiftly slapped her arms away and shoved her to the floor.

Adele is thrown off when he twists and lunges his torso forward. Adele backed up, she shot upward as the gangster approached her.

"We saved your life."

"This has nothing to do with you," he growled.

The gangster lunged at Adele. Grabbing her, she did everything she could to break free of his grip but he was obviously too strong.

Brianna had to stop this but what could she do? From the brief glimpses of Adele's struggle, even Adele could not beat him. She needed something to give them an advantage. They had no weapons, all they had were medical supplies.

Medical supplies…syringes and drugs…

Brianna quickly got up and rushed over to a drawer while Dillion was still struggling to drag Adele off of the floor. She opened the drawer and pulled out a syringe.

Adele noticed this and turned Dillion away from Brianna so he doesn't see what's coming. Then she kicked Dillon in the crotch and he let go of her.

Brianna took up a dosage of the sedative from the vial. Her hands were shaky. She paused to calm herself and while he was still screaming from the pain inflicted on him by Adele, Brianna stuck the syringe into his neck, emptying the content into his body.

"Ah!" Dillon yells and dropped to the floor, completely motionless.

"Sedative. Get him out of here," Brianna said dismissingly. Brianna would drop unto the floor in exhaustion but she immediately turned to Kelvin.

"And put him where? I'm not gonna be able to carry him," Adele groaned rubbing her neck where she had been held.

Brianna helped Kelvin up and put him on the bed. "Drag him into a room and lock it from the outside."

Adele grabbed Dillon by the ankles and with all the strength she could muster, she drags him along the tile floor out of the room. "Come on you big bastard."

"I'm so sorry. You won't see him again."

Brianna looked at the injuries. Two holes had been reopened. It has not been too bad. But Kelvin was bleeding and the injuries could easily get infected.

"He just got the stitching. I'll sow you back up. You're gonna be fine." Brianna says as she begins to gather the supplies she'll need.

Kelvin tried to gain his composure. Brianna felt the urge to ask. "What did you do to him? Or, what does he think you did?"

"It's not me. It's my people," he responded knowing she had questions.

Brianna frowned at that. Everyone knew most of the killings in the street were by association. If they cannot find the actual person, they will attack your babymother, friends or family. That was the way of the streets.

Kelvin will be in danger even when he leaves. Brianna pushed out those negative thoughts as she treads the needle and was about to pierce the skin. Brianna had to hope he will be ok. She had to have hope.

"I will patch you up, he won't be a problem anymore."

Kelvin's mouth opened but he said nothing. Brianna knew he was afraid. She was as well. She hid it well but she almost lost herself to the wraith of fear a minute ago.

He could have hurt them badly. Right now, her left ribs were throbbing in pain. A few cuts along her arms and a pain in the back of her head. She kept the concentration to continue her job effortlessly sewing up one hole.

She wiped the blood from that with a gauze. She moved over the next hole, sliding the needle into the skin, he winces. She really hoped Malvin could find someone.

CHAPTER 13

The sun was beaming brightly. The wind whistled a rising crescendo that held the attention blocking out the random noise that picked at Malvin's ear; Huge crowd, it flowed through the main doors. A constant stream in either direction, it really gave weight to the number of people at this place. The marquee suggests that it is a bodybuilder convention.

Among the crowd, Melvin entered. Melvin stood just inside. He looked around taking in his surroundings. There were some booths depicting pictures of martial arts in action. People in dojo clothes, Malvin figured those were self-defense clubs. He wondered if those were places, he could go to for help. But would they be receptive to that he wondered?

Malvin was not sure they were the people he should approach. They may not be so good at self-defense. He had to pick the right place or should he pick the right person, he figured?

He wavered his eyes around and picked out a lot of big guys. Muscles thick and powerfully built, they were like giants. Malvin did not want to get in their way.

He would be flattened.

But can they fight? I need to find someone. I can't walk up to a group of people. I need to find someone who seems strong but can probably fight his way out of many situations. But how I figure out if any of these big guys can fight?

Melvin stood in one corner, people watching.

A nicely built man stepped out of the crowd and took a moment to look at his phone. The man was standing a few feet from Malvin. Malvin sized the man with his eyes, trying hard to avoid any eye contact.

Should I go over? I mean he seems strong enough. Still, how do I ask him to join us? Should I just offer a security job off the bat or should I talk about the responsibility it entails?

Malvin fidgeted in distraught as he wondered if he should approach. He had to do something. He came here for a reason, better to do it now. He finally walked over to the man.

The man felt eyes on him and glanced at Melvin's direction. "Hi," Malvin blurted out before he could think.

"Hi," the nicely built man replied.

"I have a question. Maybe you can answer it for me."

"Sure." The man put away his phone.

"I'm looking for a person, preferably a man. A strong man. Someone with a certain set of skills."

"You mean - like a male prostitute?" he asked with a blank expression.

"No. God, no. Um - sorry. Never mind." Malvin quickly walked away afraid that he might have caused a scene.

That did not go well at all. I am really struggling to find someone. What do I do now? Should I approach one of those martial artists?

Malvin peeked a look back. The man had taken out his phone again. He didn't seem phased by the question he was just asked. At least he was tougher than Malvin took him for.

Get yourself together, you can do this.

His thoughts went back to what that gangster Dillion said. Right now, Brianna and the other girls were left back there with that guy.

Malvin wondered if she was ok. He decided to call her.

She answers, "Got some good news, Mal?"

I have to do this.

Malvin walked away from the hustle and bustle of the convention center. "Can't say I do...I don't think this is the way to go about things. Have to do an ad. Post on Craigslist. Monster. I don't know. But not this."

"Where did you go?" Brianna asked.

Should I tell her? She would probably laugh at me.

"You still there?" Brianna asked.

"Yeah, I'm here. I just didn't want to answer you."

"Why?" she sounded offended.

"It's embarrassing."

More slowly, "Where did you go?"

"The bodybuilder convention."

"There's a bodybuilder convention?"

"Yeah, there is. It's just awkward. Even I can't go up to a complete stranger and try to offer them a job out of the blue for a bodyguard type of gig."

"Yeah. Well, get back to base. We could use you," She replied sounding worried.

Malvin nodded. "I'm leaving now." The call ends. Malvin sighed and made his way past the last four booths near the exit. He finally reached outside and the sun backed him in its intensity. As he walks through the crowd he sees further up the street, two muscular men surrounding a homeless man.

The first man said, "Get a job you bum."

The second man added, "You're probably gonna use the money for booze anyway."

Malvin was perturbed by the sight. Suddenly another man, blond wavy hair blue shirt, unbuttoned revealing the black t-shirt, he stepped close behind those two men, "Leave the guy alone," He says, facing them.

"Why don't you mind your own business?" the first man asks.

"You've got all that muscle but no brains," the new guy replied.

The first man growled in a low voice, "Whatever." Then he proceeded to slap the money cup out of the Homeless Man's hand. Both muscular men laugh as they walked away. Malvin slowed down hoping they don't notice him as he neared the scene.

The new guy twirled with a scowl on his face. "Where you guys going?"

The men don't answer.

"I said, where are you guys going? You've got change to pick up," the new guy spoke.

The bullies stopped and turn around.

"We ain't picking up shit," the second guy said.

"I think you should." The new guy replied, his confidence intriguing.

The bullies looked at each other. They started to walk towards the new guy.

"Is that right? You gonna make us?" the second guy asked, laughing.

The new guy rocked his head. "If I have to."

Both the bullies laughed.

The second man pushes the new guy but he doesn't fall, rather he pushes back really hard. Malvin notices a crowd slowing to watch the situation unfold.

"You gonna tell us to pick up the change again?" the first man stepped up.

The new guy stood straight and spoke with gusto. "Well, you still haven't yet, so yes. Pick it up."

The two men cracked their knuckles. Malvin is shaken with fear.

The second man swung at the new guy. He ducked the punch. In one beautiful motion, the new guy hit both men and seized the second one in a painful arm hold. He dropped to one knee in pain.

The new guy aptly joked, "While you're down there might as well pick up the change."

The first man recoiled. He grabbed his nose, his face scrunched up in pain. His eyes went wild watching the new guy beating on his friend. The first man spoke unsure, "Let him go."

The new guy drew back the man's arm, the second bully screamed. "It'll cost him," The new guy replied smoothly.

The second bully began to pick up all the change quickly. His palm postured towards the new guy with the change. The new guy grabbed the change and let go of the man's arm.

"Payment received," the new guy replied with a mischievous smirk on his face.

The second bully stood up with a pronounced frown. The new guy stood there staring at them. Both men traded wary glances, they recognized this was not a fight they could win and quickly walked away.

The new guy approached the homeless man. Though the homeless man shrunk back a bit, once the new guy laid out his hand with the change, "I believe this is yours."

The homeless man moved forward and grabbed up the change gingerly in his cupped hands. Once the Homeless Man was done taking his money, the new guy walked away without even looking back.

Malvin who had been watching from the side was impressed. "Sir!" He yelled trying to get the attention of the new guy. "Can I talk to you for a minute?"

The new guy turned. He stared hard at Malvin, Malvin slightly shaken by the stare relaxed his shoulders and breathed out to get his confidence up and to avoid it cracking. "What you did was amazing."

The new guy widened his eyes at Malvin. "Oh, well, hmm ok thanks."

"I mean…ah listen let me buy you a drink."

The new guy tilted his head as he gave Malvin an odd stare.

"I am Malvin, and you are?"

"Sam,"

"Nice to meet you, I really respect what you did. Many people do things but never get rewarded for it. You did a good thing. I am Malvin," he replied, rushing his words to avoid choking.

Sam returned the handshake with a smirk on his face. "Thanks, I guess. But they were not that difficult to deal with. You don't need to buy me anything," He replied.

Malvin did not want to lose him right now, he still wanted to offer the job to him. "I insist."

Sam grabbed the back of his neck with a nervous smile blooming. "Alright, I will take you up on your offer."

They went to the bar across the street. They have a seat at a table. Malvin helped Sam get his drink. "Thanks," Sam replied as he took a sip.

"Why do it?" Malvin asks, starting up a discussion.

"Cause it was the right thing to do," Sam replied flatly.

"Exactly. Sam. What do you do for a living?"

Sam hesitated but finally said, "Work for a temp agency."

"Is that your life's calling? Being a temp."

Sam shrugged, "Is it anybody's?"

"If you could do anything. Anything in the world. What would it be?"

"I don't know. I never had a skill."

"There has to be something," Malvin urged.

"Probably do something that helped people I guess."

"I was hoping you'd say that."

Sam quirked an eyebrow at Malvin then asked, "What do you do?"

"I'm part of a team that helps people that can't find help anywhere else."

Sam smiled instantly. "You're an Avenger?"

They both burst out laughing.

"That would be cool," Malvin paused to catch his breath. "But no. We do work the streets though."

Sam rocked his head in thought. "What does that have to do with me? Are you guys sort of like underground cops or something?"

"Haha. No, we are not any of that. We're looking for someone to join the team. Someone with a particular set of skills," Malvin replied, relieved that Sam had a sense of humor.

"Sounds like you're looking for Bryan Mills."

"I don't think I've got to look any further. I found the guy. Sam…" Malvin doesn't know Sam's last name and was rolling his wrist hoping Sam would fill him in.

"Dryer," Sam answered back.

"Sam Dryer. What do you say?" Sam took some of his drink and stared blankly at the cabinet contemplatively. "I guess it would be a lie if I said my interest wasn't piqued."

Malvin beamed happily. He lifted his glass before Sam. "That's a starting point." They raised their glasses in a toast before taking another drink.

CHAPTER 14

Brianna and Adele entered the room. Kelvin laid in bed trying to get some rest but his eyes were slightly open. It wavered towards them when they stepped in. They were both tired and slightly demotivated. Even though they subdued the gangster, he was a strong guy and this was an old building he could easily break down the door if he wanted.

"How are you feeling?" Brianna asked.

"Like human swiss cheese," Kelvin said flashing a quick smile.

"Glad you still can find your sense of humor," Brianna said. Unlocking the breaks on his bed, they were had to move him out of this room and place him in the staff area. It had a keypad; it was more secure. Granted it was risky, that was where the storeroom and their living quarters was but they did not want to risk putting him in any more danger.

It was their fault that the other guy was here anyways. They had to do their best to manage the situation until they get someone to help with security. Adele went behind the bed while Brianna held the opposite end. Brianna pulled as Adele steered it.

"What are you doing? Kelvin asked.

"We're going to take you to a safer area," Brianna said.

"Somewhere your friend can't get you."

Kevin nodded, resting his head deeper on the pillow.

Brianna started to pull the bed towards the room's door. Brianna and Adele guided Kevin's bed down the hall. They pass the room where he was still locked in.

As they walk past, the gangster kept hitting the glass at the top of the door. "Where you takin' him!?"

Brianna got flustered but quickly roused some anger. "Away from you," Brianna said.

"I'mma get you," the gangster shouts at Kelvin. Adele rolled her eyes. The bed moved past the room and out of the gangster's view.

"Don't worry. We're not gonna let that happen," Brianna said.

Kelvin nodded in understanding but he looked uneasy nevertheless. Brianna hoped she could keep her promise and really protect him. They carried him into an elevator and from there they reached a bare, complete empty apartment. This looked like it was recently renovated. They were planning to expand this into another room for the organization.

"One of the best views in the city. Would you like a spot over by the window?"

"Sure," Kelvin replied.

They rolled the bed towards the window, parking it a few feet away. From here he can see most of the Atlanta skyline. Brianna and Adele locked the wheels on either side of the bed.

They went back for his monitors and painstakingly plugged them back up.

Brianna looked towards Adele. "Stay with him until Mary Jane gets here. When she does, we'll venture out."

Adele nodded slightly. Brianna headed for the door. Brianna wanted to check up on April. She was doing well so far. Angelic told Brianna that April has not been too desperate for a fix. April had been obediently following the regiment.

Brianna was surprised but she knew April was determined to beat her addiction. She was making an effort which is rare among many recovering addicts. Though Brianna surmised whatever stress pushed April to use must have been external. April being here was for best for her to avoid her being near those stressors.

Brianna opened the door and saw April pacing the room. April stopped, looked up with wide almost wild eyes. Brianna froze in concern. "Everything okay?" Brianna asked.

"Yeah. Just feeling bored."

Brianna nodded. "How about we get some fresh air?"

April followed Brianna upstairs, they reached quick enough to feel the soft thick breeze of the morning. April relaxed and paced more slowly on the empty roof. She hung by the edge admiring the city below. Brianna realized it had been a long time she had been up here. Well, there was not much up here other than exhaust fans boxed in for the air conditioners below. Brianna smirked at her boot unsettling the thick dirt that settled like a coat of filthy snow. They might need a cleaner too now that she thought of it. Angelic pretty much did that and they helped her out from time to time. But even Brianna knew this place was very large and there was not a lot of manpower to deal with most of the rooms.

Brianna decided she would bring that idea to Malvin's attention when he came back. Taking in the view of the city April took a few deep breaths. Soaking up the sun, they stood there in peaceful silence.

"See you're feeling better," Brianna said.

"For now, I know it's not going to last," April answered.

"It will, once you break the addiction."

"I haven't felt good without the help of some sort of drug since…well, since I can remember."

"I know what you mean."

"You do?" April asked looked back at Brianna a little shocked. "I'm sure you've treated other people like me. You've seen it but you can't know what it's really like unless you've experienced it."

Brianna doesn't say anything. She did not want to talk about that part of her history. It was a disgraceful time in her opinion. A time Brianna felt like she was at her weakest.

"You were an addict?" April knew addiction well, so much so she could read it off Brianna's face and demeanor.

Brianna tried to push the emotion down as she replied, "We've all done things we're not proud of."

"You don't seem like someone who'd do drugs."

"Well, you should be in good spirits then."

"What'd ya mean?"

"I can help you to become the same way."

April nodded in understanding and smiled. "That's why I'm here."

"It's going to get tough. There will be times when the easier thing to do is just get high again. You've gotta really want it."

"I do. What made you want to get clean?"

Brianna wondered if she should mention her mother, the time she was left for dead.

No, that would be a loaded gun of a conversation. Besides, I have to give April positivity at this point, not guilt that will push her on the wrong path.

She turned and looked at April. "How about we save that for another time? If you stick it out. The whole way through. We'll be spending enough time together to share all kinds of stories."

"I'm going to hold you to it."

"And I, you."

CHAPTER 15

A well-lit office, commendations, and pictures lined the walls. Behind the dark wood table with a mini US flag was the Police Chief, in his sixties.

"Where do you think he is?" the Police Chief asked Detective Gray.

"I don't know. Not yet. Can I say where I hope he is?" Detective Gray leaned forward, "Dead."

"What do you know?" The Chief asked.

"I know there was someone in the house that was hurt pretty bad. We're checking the local hospitals now. Two dead. Both bodies left on the porch. Each had the other's wallet in their pocket."

"Why do you think that was?"

"Maybe this was a robbery. Neither wallet had any cash."

"Be a pretty bold robbery wouldn't you say?"

"I was thinking stupid. But bold is another way to put it."

"What's the next move you had in mind?"

"If the hospitals don't check out, a full city search. Both men. The one in the house and the one in the car have to within close range. Maybe someone will tip us off on their whereabouts. Anyone around here could use the reward money." Detective Gray remembered something, "One person. A next-door neighbor said they saw a black van out front just minutes after the shooting. When the cops arrived, it wasn't there. We're looking into that as well."

"Alright get to it Detective Gray, we need to solve this and move on to other things."

"Yes sir," Detective Gray replied.

Detective Gray left the chief's office and made his way outside. He sat in his car, started up the engine and jumped the police radio as the car purred to satisfaction.

An officer's voice is heard over the police radio. "We are in position. Waiting for your command."

"Remember. The car was registered to a person in this house which means he should be considered armed and dangerous."

"Ten-four," the officer replied.

"Proceed," Detective Gray said.

The raid should go off without a hitch. Hopefully, the person who the vehicle is registered to is in the house the SWAT team is raiding. Detective Gray rolled off into the city and made his way to the scene.

The inner city with its poor broken-down apartments, and dreary houses on badly patched grass, he hated rolling into this place without backup. It was not that he was scared but a lone cop was a target not a threat to the evil elements there. He knew that much.

As he came close to the house, he saw the crowd gathered like a swarm around the house. He blew his horn and they parted. He stopped in front of the house. SWAT team members exited the house with several men in handcuffs. They led them to police vehicles that now line the street out front.

Detective Gray watched the scene. One of the SWAT team members, who was not escorting anyone, walked up to Detective Gray. "House is clear. Not sure exactly who we have. We'll take care of that down at the station."

"Everyone okay?" Detective Gray asked.

"Yes. We're all accounted for and no injuries on either side."

"Nice work. Still, I want to talk to the one who owns the car."

The SWAT member left, he talked to the others. After some minutes he returned and pointed at one car. Detective Gray mouthed a thank you and went over. He opened up the back door of the police cruiser.

Sitting inside cuffed, was Terrence, the man Gray been looking to talk to. "You Terrence?"

"I ain't talking to no police. I ain't no snitch," Terrance retorted.

"It'd be smart if you did. Might be able to save your friend's life." Detective Gray looked at him but he did not react. Detective Gray continued, "The car, riddled with bullet holes, abandoned in an alley. It's registered to you. I'm gonna make an educated guess and say you were driving it when one of your buddies got pretty hurt. Looked like he was bleeding all over the place."

"What you trying to say?" Terrence asked.

"More of asking. Where is he? Where did he go?"

"I don't know."

"You don't know or just don't want to tell me?"

Terrence didn't answer.

"Right now, I'm more concerned about his wellbeing than what he may have or didn't do. Did he get medical attention somewhere?"

Terrence shrugged still saying nothing.

"Where did he go?"

"Look. I have no idea. We all went in our separate directions after it happened."

Detective Gray smiled. "So, you were there?"

Terrence threw his head against the headrest, upset that he just gave himself out.

"If you do care about your brother, you better hope he found some help and we don't find him lying in a ditch somewhere."

Detective Gray stepped out and shut the door.

CHAPTER 16

The front door swung open. Brianna was hiding behind the dishware cabinet. She was really happy her father was here. "Where's Brianna?" she heard him ask.

"Bri! Your dad's here!"

Young Brianna, happy-go-lucky twelve-year-old, rushed towards the door. "Daddy!" Brianna knew him as Tim. That was his name. Her mother's name was Kelly. She wished they could be together like it used to be.

But things were different and Brianna only could see her father some times. Brianna gives her dad a hug. He hugs her back. "Go get your things." Brianna runs back into the house and up the steps.

"You knew it was my weekend. She should already have her stuff ready," her father's voice thundered. Brianna froze just behind the wall at the top of the stairs.

"You better take good care of her," Kelly fired back.

"I do. You look terrible."

"You don't get to judge me."

"It's not a judgment if it's true. You shouldn't be doing that stuff at all - let alone, around my daughter."

They are having a fight.

Brianna jumped off the wall and ran to the room, quickly grabbed her bag. Brianna comes back down the stairs and rushed to stand by her father's side.

Her father looked down at her with wide eyes, with a sigh he looked up. "Say bye to mom."

"Bye, mom."

Kelly replied, "You behave and listen to your father."

"I know."

Tim and Brianna headed for his truck parked in front of the house. Tim drove out onto the road.

"How you doin', dad?" Brianna replied.

"How am I doing? Hun, I'm your father. I should be the one making sure you're okay."

They both laughed. They decided to start their time together with some food.

Yes, I am with daddy. I wish mother was here. But she is always somewhere else. Not like she was somewhere else; I mean she was there but it was like she was not there. It...how do I even think about this properly? Not even sure how and why. But when she argues with daddy it always ends badly. Why do they have to argue? When I talk with daddy, we don't argue. When I talk with mommy, we don't argue.

Well, they shout at me, mommy especially. But that is usually when I do something stupid. I have not done anything stupid in a while though. But that is because I am a good girl!

Young Brianna and her father bought burgers, fries and a side order of potato wedges. They were enjoying the food when Tim asked, "How's everything at home?"

"Okay. I guess," Brianna answered.

"I only expect great things for my daughter. Why's it only okay?"

"Cause you're not there with us."

Her father stared at her wordless for a while. "Bri. I'm sorry. Sometimes things happen."

"Like what?"

"Things you're too young to know about."

"Why can't I live with you?"

"That's something I ask myself. I'm working on it. Why? Don't want you to live with mom?"

"She's always sleeping. When she's not she's either yelling or not there. What's wrong with her?"

"Your mom's got problems."

She sipped her drink and grabbed up some fries in her hand. "What problems?"

"Problems you're too young to worry about."

Brianna was getting frustrated. She was used to this but it was getting tiring. "Is that going to be your answer to everything?"

Her father giggled, "I don't know. Do you have more of the same questions?"

"Not if that's going to be the go-to answer."

They continued eating.

"I want you to worry about you. Not your mom. Not even me. We're adults. We should be able to take care of ourselves. You just need to do you."

Young Brianna smiled and gulped all the fries in her hand.

"Got it?" he asked.

Brianna looked at the empty container that once had so many fries. She nodded and said, "Got it." She laid out her open palm, "Give me some of your fries." Tim looked at Brianna curiously.

"Taking your advice, dad," she said. He shook his head and chuckles.

Young Brianna and Tim exited the restaurant and began walking down the street.

"What are we doing now?" Brianna asked.

"Well, I thought we could have some fun."

"What kind of fun?"

"There's a new arcade that opened up just down the street from here."

"Really!?"

"That something you'd be interested in checking out?" Young Brianna enthusiastically shook her head yes.

Tim takes out his wallet from his back pocket. Removed a twenty-dollar bill, hands it to Young Brianna.

"How many games do you think we'll be able to play with that?" he asked.

"Probably like all of em."

"At least a couple of times," he said, correcting her.

Tim and Brianna walked past a homeless man sitting against a trash can. Wrapped in deep brown rags, a hat hid a good portion of his face but as he looked up it was rather rosy with spots of black smudges on the side. He holds out a cup, shook it.

"Spare change?" the homeless beggar asked.

Tim stops walking and Young Brianna followed his lead.

"Sorry. I've got nothing on me," he said to the beggar.

Tim looked at Brianna.

Brianna looked at the Beggar. She then looks down at the twenty-dollar bill in her fist.

Think about me, right? Me first, I should do me.

Brianna looked towards the Beggar. "Nope." Brianna started to walk away with a little skip.

Brianna wavered her head around and finally saw the brightly-lit neon purple sign.

Jacker's Funland…funny name.

The door was high, bulbs on the side. The wall was painted red with picturesque images of kids in play. She could hear children screaming, synthetic noises like the chorus to a wild song. But it would seem this was the right place.

Brianna was about to step in when she felt a strong tug. She leaped around in fright. Tim, her father had grabbed her.

"What are you doing, dad?" Brianna asked. She noted that he looked upset. Did she do something?

"What was that back there?" he asked.

"What was what?"

"Don't play dumb with me. That might work with your mother, but not me."

Brianna crinkled her brow in wonder and thought back.

Oh, it must have to do with that guy he was standing in front of.

"I just said no to the guy."

"That's not like you. That's not what the daughter I know would have done."

"What would I have usually have done?"

"You would have helped that man."

"That money you gave me is for the arcade. It's for me."

"Didn't you see that the man needed your help. You could have helped him. Made a difference in his day. Maybe his life."

Brianna was struggling to understand this. She looked at her money then she replied, "I've gotta just do me."

"What?"

"I've just gotta look after myself. Like you said. And I want to have fun at the arcade."

Tim took a deep breath. "Maybe I said it wrong. That's not what I meant."

Brianna stared in blank confusion.

"I want you to do what makes you happy. I want you to follow your heart. That good heart you have inside of you. I know your mom isn't like she used to be. I know I'm not around all the time like I use to be. That's from the mistakes we made. I don't want you to make those same mistakes. I want you to be you and worry about you because you're the best of your mom and I. That's what I was trying to say. You do you, cause when you are, there's nobody better."

Brianna had a tear in her eye. She looked towards the Arcade, then back at her father. Brianna knew what she had to do. Brianna went back, her father following her all the way. She placed the twenty-dollar bill in the Homeless man's cup.

The man began to cry, a tear cleaved through the dirt on his face leaving a pale river through which she could see who he was before the hardship. "Thank you so much. You're a sweet angel."

"You're welcome," Brianna answered him back.

Her father patted her on her head, "Let's go."

Tim and Young Brianna walked away.

"That man could be you. Wouldn't you want someone to help you in your time of need."

Brianna smiled and nods her head yes.

"Think the Arcade has an ATM?"

Brianna smiled wider.

At least I still get to play at the arcade. Yaaaaay!

Brianna jolts awake from her daydreaming. She often had these reoccurring dreams where she was back to her childhood, and each time felt more real than the previous one. She guessed she was probably having the dreams because she was doing something that stemmed from the teachings she got from her parents.

CHAPTER 17

The gangster was still locked in the room. Sitting on the floor, he seemed calm. Brianna wondered if he really was. She did not want to go in and have him attack her. But she wanted to help him because she knew at this point that he must be hungry.

She could not leave him there. Brianna resolved to face him. Brianna unlocks the door and steps into the room.

He remained seated. Actually, he did not look at her.

She began, "Two questions. One. You settled down?" He said nothing. "Two. You Hungry?" He finally looked. It was an icy stare that said much without any words. Brianna could feel the weight of something deeper in his stare.

He breathed out and looked away. "Alright."

"Come on then. You can follow me."

She brought him to a room that was decently sized. Long tables fill one side of the room. On the other, a large kitchen area, sitting at one table was Dillon and Brianna. She found out his name was Dillion with what little small talk she could make. Dillon seemed to not be angry at them even though they sedated him.

Brianna was glad. He was indifferent right now but she knew getting in his way will be to her detriment. Dillon was eating a sandwich, a glass of water to assist him.

Without looking at her, "You know you can't keep me locked up like that."

Brianna was shaken but she tried to put on a strong front. "As long as you're here you'll play by our rules. Go nuts on another patient like that and you'll be locked right back up. You're free to go any time you'd like. But with your injuries, it's gonna be hard running away from the cops once you leave."

"I hear ya," Dillion replied.

Mary Jane entered.

Brianna nodded at her. She stood up from the table. "When you're done you can go back to your regular room."

Brianna put her hand on his shoulder for a moment. He did not react he just kept eating. She nodded and walked over to Mary Jane.

Brianna joined Mary Jane at the doorway leading out of that room.

"How's everything going today?" Mary Jane asked.

Brianna lowered her voice. "Had a little incident."

"Medical?"

"Physical." Brianna turned her head towards Dillon to make sure he couldn't hear her. "He decided to rip open a few of Kelvin's stitches."

Mary Jane's jaw dropped, "Why would he do that?

"Some type of beef. I moved him upstairs. That's where Adele is now. We're going to do our nightly round but I wanted to wait until you got here."

"You gonna go now?"

"Once you've settled in."

"I'm good. I'll go tell Adele to come down."

"Double check his stitch work. Should be fine but I'm not as good as you when it comes to that stuff."

"Sure."

Mary Jane almost walked away but swiftly remembering something she stops. "Oh. Got the check."

"Great. Same amount?" Brianna asked.

"No. More."

"How much more?

"Hundred thousand."

"Wow. That's a ton more."

"It does come with a string attached. We'll talk about it when you get back."

Mary Jane walked away.

Brianna couldn't imagine what it would be but Mary Jane doesn't appear concerned so she doesn't bother to worry about it either. Brianna went to fetch Adele who was napping.

Brianna knocked on the wall of the room which stuttered Adele out of her slumber. "Wake up sleepyhead."

Adele opened her eyes quite slowly. "Do I look like a child to you?" she answered rolling her eyes.

Brianna giggled and replied, "Let us go out for a street run. You got the energy up for it?"

Adele yawned. Shot up she twisted off the bed and swiftly walked to the door. "Whenever you are, let me wash my face," Adele said. Brianna smiled.

Brianna went out to the front, where she saw Angelic at her post. Brianna leaned over on the countertop.

"Adele and I will be stepping out for a while. Need anything? Something happens, don't hesitate to call. Should only be gone the usual couple of hours," Brianna said.

"Will do," Angelic replied.

"Do your rounds. Hopefully, Mal is back soon."

Brianna walked to the exit and saw Adele. "Ready to go?"

"Yep," Adele said.

Brianna turned around briefly, and said to Angelic, "Alright. See you later."

"Bye, ladies. Stay safe."

Brianna and Adele exited the building and down the steps to the black van that's parked on the curb.

Adele drove them into the heart of the city. They reached a place around an abandoned apartment. The back alley in this district was big and had a burnt down mini-mart. Many homeless lived here. This was a spot where the veterans on the streets congregated and where new ones freshly introduced to this life looked for some form of guidance on how to live.

Adele and Brianna walked down the narrow path between two broken-down buildings. The path quickly opened up into this bare plaza which was nothing more than a patchy road that led from behind the minimart. The platform that held the two metal glider doors was high and afforded the homeless that slept on there an avoidance of the suspicious cars that come through from time to time.

Each person had made their home out of something, whether it be a box, sheets, old furniture. Resourcefulness was a very important skill to have out here. For the nurses, to see this first hand it broke their hearts a bit but at least they were doing their part to help make it better for the homeless.

Adele and Brianna were given a chorus of good mornings and waves. Cries of joy at their arrival, Brianna nodded and started asking who needed what. Adele started bandaging up an older homeless woman's arm that had a serious-looking cut on it.

Brianna listened to another homeless woman's heartbeat with her stethoscope. "Just breathe normally." Brianna listened carefully. "Lungs sound find. Good news."

The woman smiled.

Brianna looked around and saw a homeless man hobbling over to his makeshift home. His back was facing her but it was his right leg that concerned her. He seemed to be struggling to fully place it on the ground. He was tiptoeing on it and she could see from his shivering body that it hurt him each time. She walked over to the man.

"Sir. Sir. Are you okay?"

The man turned around and Brianna recognized him, Aaron.

"The limp looks like it is getting worse," Brianna said, with a knowing look.

"You remember me?"

"Of course. It was only earlier today."

He looked away. "Most people don't pay attention to us."

"Can I please take a look at it?"

"I'm fine. I saw online, all I have to do is ice it."

Brianna was surprised. "Where do you have the internet?"

"The library."

Brianna thought for a second. "That's like a mile or two away from here. You walked all that way?"

"It was nothing."

Brianna was more concerned now. "Well, did you put ice on it?"

Aaron gave a dismissive nod. "I would if I had any."

"Aaron. Sit down and let me look at it."

Aaron hesitated for a bit and finally gave in. He sat down on the pavement and hikes his pants leg up. He was not wearing any socks. The swelling had gotten even worse.

"You could have a broken ankle," Brianna said noting how disfigured the ball of the ankle looked in proportion to where it should be.

"I'll live."

Brianna stared at him. This man was being too stubborn for his own good. "In terrible pain?"

"Just another day."

Brianna could see he was used to being ignored all his life. He must be a new one around here at least. His mindset won't shift with one act of kindness. But she understood his distrust and lack of hope. In this life, you had to accept the hopelessness of the circumstances rather than makeup dreams that will never occur. But she was resolved to give him hope for today at least. "Stay here."

Brianna rushed back to the van. She opened up the igloo. Inside were flat rectangular plastic containers. They were all filled with water, frozen inside. Around the containers were packs of ice in bags.

She took out one large container pack and took a small bag for good measure. Returning to his rather surprised reaction, she laid the plastic container in his hands. He shivered with the instant cold he felt.

"Place it on your ankle I am going to wrap it," she told him.

Aaron held the large ice pack on his swollen ankle as Brianna wraps it with a bandage to keep it in place.

She pointed at his leg. "Try and stay off your feet, at least this one for a few days."

"Seeing as I don't really have anywhere to go that shouldn't be a problem."

Brianna stared at him as she pursed her lips. "If you want help getting back on your feet..."

"Metaphorically or physically?"

"Either. Or both. Just ask. I'll do whatever I can," she said with a smile.

"Thanks for the offer."

"So that's a no to both?"

Aaron opened his mouth but quickly closed it, shook his head and looked away. "I don't like handouts. I will be just fine on my own."

"It's not a handout. You'd have to do the work. I'd just help you face the right direction."

"Thanks. You've already done more than enough. I'm nobody special."

"Neither am I."

He smirked and with a wave of hand said, "You look after all of us. I've seen you around before. Day and night. In the middle of summer. Heart of winter. You're the special one."

Brianna blushed as Aaron smiled.

"Aren't you a charmer?" Brianna said as she stood up. "I'll check up on you in a few days. Take care of yourself."

Aaron nods. Brianna walked away toward the van. Helping people like Aaron, people who thought they'd been long forgotten by society and didn't matter at all was what really gives her a sense of value.

CHAPTER 18

Brianna sat in the passenger seat filling out how much supplies she had used, who they were used on, notable changes and follow-ups. Brianna was glad things were working out. With extra funding they could do more for people in need, that would mean they might need more workers. It was hard enough for them to do this as it was.

Damn, we only realize now how much we need new people. I really should place an ad out.

Adele entered the van and took a seat behind the wheel as she waited to turn on the engine. Brianna continued doing paperwork feeling Adele's eyes on her.

"You know we don't have to do paperwork. Most of the people we see, we see once, and then never again."

"I know. It's just the way I like to do things."

"Almost done?"

"Almost."

"Good. I need some sleep."

"Might want to stay up for a little while longer."

Adele stared annoyingly at Brianna. Brianna put down her paperwork and looked back at Adele. Brianna decided to tell her what was on our mind. "Mary Jane said our donor wants to give us an extra hundred thousand."

"Hundred thousand? As in one, zero, zero, zero, zero, zero?" Adele asked in shock.

Brianna almost laughed. "Yep."

"What for?"

"I don't know. But we can do a ton with that much money."

Brianna saw Adele's eyes lighting up with excitement.

"Hospital could use it," Brianna replied.

"Oh."

Brianna detected Adele's disappointment. "What?"

"I thought maybe we could use that to give us an actual paycheck," Adele said.

Well, it was not like they could not get paid but right now it would be difficult to maintain cost. So, each person was paid a small commission but only on payment or donation received from any outcalls. So, the person could take a cut from any money received from working on that outcall. Other than that, there was a stipend but that was primarily for food. It was not much to live off on.

But Brianna was ok with that, "Everything we need. Housing. Food. That's taken care of. That's what's so great about this gig."

Adele glared then suddenly looked ahead. "Don't you ever just want a break? Go on a vacation?"

"Who would I go with? You don't need a break if you're doing something you love."

Adele turned on the van's engine.

"Mary Jane did say though that there was a catch."

"Isn't there always when it comes to money?" Adele shifted the car into drive.

Brianna shrugged. They moved off and drove back to the hospital. They walked into the hospital and joined Angelic at her post.

"Is Mary Jane still with Kevin?" Brianna asked Angelic.

"Yes."

"Let's go up and let her know we're back," Brianna said.

Adele nodded.

Brianna almost moved, looking back she said, "Any problems?"

Angelic shook her head. "None. It's been very peaceful."

Brianna was glad and nervous at the same time. She prematurely asked, "Really?"

"Listen," Angelic said with a wave of her arms.

There was no noise whatsoever. Brianna moved away from the counter content.

Walked down the hall, Adele decided to crash. Brianna who was a bit restless lingered out in the hall in thought. She wondered who she should check on first, she could find out how April was doing. Brianna looked into April's room and sees April in bed sleeping.

Nah, I will see Dillion first maybe getting to know him a little better I can try to calm that rage in him. Brianna looked into Dillon's room. It's empty. A surge of contention rife with shock befuddled her. Brianna turned and looked back at the front desk. "Where's Dillon!"

"He's not there!?" Angelic called.

Not again!

Brianna ran back towards the front desk. Brianna heard heavy thumps behind her, she saw that it was Adele who must have heard the exchange. Her face was mean and her stride was smooth. They started moving towards the stairwell door.

Adele punched in the code on the keypad. The door opened. Brianna went to speak to Adele about being careful but Adele cuts her off.

"I already know what you're about to say," Adele said.

CHAPTER 19

Malvin was walking with Sam. They were walking towards the hospital. To say Malvin was happy was an understatement. He knew Sam was exactly what they needed; he could feel it in his gut.

Yes, finally we found somebody. Trust might still be something to consider but I really think he is a good enough guy and he really wants to help people. I know that much.

Melvin looked up at Sam, "When you get there you will meet everybody. Brianna. She's basically our leader. She'll be able to answer any questions you might have. You can check out what we're all about and see if it's something you'd want to be a part of."

Sam tilted his head side to side contemplating what Malvin said. "I'm not making any promises," He replied.

Malvin and Sam entered the building. Sam was already throwing glances of disbelief at Malvin and hesitated. It was like with each glance he was asking, 'you sure about this?' or 'is this the right place?'"

Malvin smiled at him and confidently moved forward. He was used to that. Most people in the medical industry scrunched up their noses at them just as easily.

"I know what you're thinking. This place looks terrible. It's kinda by design. Follow me," led Sam into the stairwell.

Just as Malvin and Sam entered, Adele was running up the steps.

"Where you running to?" Malvin asked.

"We've got a problem," Adele replied, panting and suddenly running off. Malvin and Sam trailed behind her confusion written all over their face.

Down the stairwell and into the hall, they are all running toward Kelvin's room.

"Stop!" Brianna suddenly screamed, bringing everyone to a halt.

Malvin, Adele, and Sam entered the room. Malvin froze to see Brianna cupped her eye socket, her legs squirming in anguish. Mary Jane was out cold on the ground. Kelvin was on the bed coughing, hand on his throat, fear in his eyes.

Adele's face puffed up, and her brow tilted heavily down as she snarled. "We should have never helped you."

Dillon does a facial shrug. "Too late."

Adele advances toward him, but Dillon kicks her feet out from under her sweeping her. She hits the ground hard on her back.

Malvin is scared she must have broken a bone or two. He wished he could do something but he couldn't face up to this guy. Malvin looks at Sam and begs, "You've gotta stop him."

Sam nodded and stepped forward.

Dillon isn't in the least fazed by Sam as he lazily gestures with a flick of his hand at Sam. "What are you going to do?"

Sam slows his steps; Dillon steps forward taking advantage and then he swung a fist at Sam. Sam ducked and grabbed Dillon's arm twisting both arms behind Dillon's back.

A crunching sound had his teeth clattering as Dillon cried out "Ahhhhh!"

Sam kicked the back of Dillon's knee and this sends him to the ground, with Sam still gripping his arm. Dillon cried out and tried to wriggle his way out of the hold but Sam held firm.

"Look, tough guy, I don't know what is going on here, but it sure looks to me like you are the bully here. These ladies you knocked out don't look like they were giving you any trouble, so I am just going to ask you nicely this one time to apologize to them and promise to never bother them again," Sam said, tightening his grip at the interval.

"Okay! Okay! Alright, I am going to apologize, but just let go of me, you are hurting me, man!" Dillion cried out.

"No. I don't trust you. Apologize to them right now," Sam fired back at him.

"I am sorry. I am sorry for hitting you guys," Dillion blurted out almost teary from the pain.

"Can you let me go now?" He yells at Sam, who loosened his grip and kicked him to the floor.

Adele picked herself up, as did Brianna. They stared at Sam with their mouths open, mesmerized by what he had just done.

"You want me to do the same thing with the other arm?" Sam asked, calmly.

"No. No. Fine. I give up," Dillon pleaded.

Sam pulled Dillon back to his feet and pushed him over to Adele, who grabbed him by the back of his shirt.

Brianna moved over to Mary Jane's side. Her head wagged side to side, regaining consciousness.

"What did you do to him?" Adele asked.

"Dislocated shoulder. You should be able to pop it back in."

Adele grinned. She nodded, clearly impressed. "Nice." She pushed Dillon towards the door she was headed for. Dillon was whimpering quite weakly.

"I thought you were big and bad," Adele said rubbing it in. They were out of sight now and Malvin was relieved.

Brianna had helped Mary Jane sit up.

"You okay?" Brianna asked.

Mary Jane looked around at them. "I don't know."

"I think you hit your head. Let's go check you out." Brianna helped Mary Jane to her feet.

Brianna walked with her towards the door. As they pass Sam, Brianna looked up at him, "Nice work. Who are you?"

"I'm Sam."

"My recruit," Malvin added.

"Can you stick around for a little while?" Brianna asked Sam.

"Sure."

Brianna continued walking away with Mary Jane. Malvin stepped over to Kelvin's bedside.

"You okay?" Malvin asked slowly.

Kelvin was rubbing his neck and groaned out an almost inaudible, "Yeah."

"I'm so sorry. That won't happen again," Malvin replied.

Kelvin rolled his eyes as he sneered, "That's what you guys said the last time."

CHAPTER 20

Mary Jane sat on an examination table. Brianna stood in front of her holding an Ophthalmoscope looking at her pupils.

After closely examining she turned off the Ophthalmoscope and hung it back on the exam room wall. "Looks like a slight concussion. Take it easy for a few days. You can stay here if you'd like," Brianna said.

"I guess. I'm gonna have to call work and tell them I'll need a few days off. Can't do procedures with a concussion," Mary Jane replied.

Mary Jane got down from the table.

Brianna pondered if now was a god time to ask Mary about that donation. With a new member coming in Brianna was not sure how the team will deal with the extra financial burden as it was. "You up to talking for a moment?" Brianna asked

"Sure. Just no brain busters,"

"Noted. What's going on with the latest donation? Why an extra hundred thousand?"

"Oh yeah, about that. The donor really thinks we're doing great work and wants us to keep it up."

"We're coming along nicely. What's the catch though? You said the bonus had a string attached."

"He wants you to get rid of the van."

"What?"

"No more house calls. At least ones that require transportation."

Brianna was shocked beyond words. She wasn't happy about this condition. The van was essential for them to get around. "Why? That doesn't make sense. Our mission is to help those that fall through the cracks. People who can't get regular medical attention."

"And that's still what we're going to do. What we can do. We just have to change the approach."

What were they to do, allow people to come here? Wouldn't that blow the whole secret thing out of the water? Well, Dillion came here but many people in the criminal underworld know about them. They can keep a secret they had to.

But a normal person, not so much, they all knew the police would not be kind to no sob story from them.

The law was the law, unauthorized medical practice was a criminal offense. Brianna remembered Kelvin, she said, "Using the van helps save lives. Look at Kelvin."

"And an extra hundred thousand will save even more."

Mary Jane walked past her. Brianna could not believe it. She was not liking this at all. Brianna feared this would happen Mary Jane stopped at the door and

they both stared at each other, Mary Jane nodded, "Think about it."

"What do you think the right call is?" Brianna asked not sure what to think.

"The van draws attention. We don't need it. The bonus money will do a lot of good."

The gears behind Brianna's eyes begin to turn. Mary Jane exited. Brianna now only had her thoughts and her thoughts were confusing and felt like a battle royal. In a way, it was probably for the best but Brianna wondered what they would do if they needed to carry patients to the hospital? That might stop. Or should they just get another vehicle? Still, it does not solve the problem. That will just become hot soon enough and equally need replacement. They had the van for a long time. It needs some conditioning right now. Getting rid of it would save that headache Brianna guessed.

Maybe we could get scooters an- No, no, that is the worse idea.

Brianna sighed and decided to think about this later. She needs to come up with an alternative to the van for now. Brianna went out to the front. She saw Malvin's and Sam's backs. They stood on the inside of the door.

In front of them was the front desk and the open hall with patient rooms on both sides.

"Impressive," Sam said.

"There's more than what you see here," Malvin replied.

"You'd never know from looking at the building on the outside that this was in here."

"That's kinda the point."

"Why?"

Brianna makes her presence known before Malvin could answer. The lights reflected off the glow of her skin as she came around and stood in front of them.

Brianna offered Sam a handshake. "That was pretty impressive up there."

Sam was only briefly surprised but nodded as he spoke, "Thanks. This place is pretty impressive."

"So, you think joining the team is something you'd be interested in?"

"I'm here. What exactly did you have in mind?"

Brianna began to answer when Adele joined them from down the hall. They all turned their attention toward her.

"Shoulder's back in." Adele smiled up at Sam. "You did a number on him. Took a while to pop it back in place."

Sam got red in the face, he nodded and tried to maintain his cool even though the accolades were beginning to make him blush.

"Where is he now?" Brianna asked with twiddling fingers.

"In his room. Locked from the outside," Adele answered.

Brianna nods.

"So, this is your recruit?" Adele asked Malvin.

"We were just talking about that," Malvin replied.

Brianna chimed in, "To answer your question. We need someone that can give us protection. We don't always deal with the nicest and well-mannered people. We don't always go to the safest places. We can do our job a lot better and have our patients be a lot more comfortable with someone with your skills around."

Sam looked flustered. He looked away as he said, "I don't know? I mean…I've always wanted to do something that pertained to really helping people. Just never seen myself as muscle."

Truly he had always wanted to be part of something that really served and helped the poor. But he was skeptical about being part of any organization because he didn't want to wake up one day and realize he had been part of a façade. He wanted to ensure that these folks were really who they said they were.

"You wouldn't be just that. We'll train you in first aid. Small procedures. You'll be helping in multiple ways," Brianna replied.

Sam nodded. "Can I sleep on it?"

"Sure."

"I'll let you know first thing tomorrow morning," Sam said.

Now that it was confirmed Sam would not be here until he made a choice it was time for them to deal more properly with their responsibility, Dillon.

"What should we do with Dillon?" Brianna asked. They looked at her gravely, their countenance moody with thoughts of the nuisance. "Can't keep him locked up forever and he's only gonna keep trying to go after Kevin for whatever reason he's got in his head."

No one answered at first, not sure how they would answer. Granted Dillon did not know Sam had left but Dillon was sneaky, he will find out soon enough.

Adele stepped forward with a solution. "We've gotta kick him out."

Brianna frowned at that. "He's not fully recovered."

"He can do that at home. He doesn't seem to care about himself anyway," Adele replied.

Malvin nods in agreement. "I agree with Adele."

Brianna really did not want to do this. She wanted to make sure he was fully recovered. She knew the police will be hounding him. But after what Dillon almost did it was too late to trust him again. "I guess you're right. I'll go..."

Adele grabbed Brianna's arm, "I'll take care of it."

Brianna was surprised by her forwardness. Still, since it was her idea, it made sense for her to be the one to execute it. "You sure?"

Adele assured her. "I'll be fine."

Adele walked away from the group and towards rooms upstairs.

Malvin turned to Sam, "I'll walk you out."

"I look forward to hearing back from you. One way or another," Brianna says before Sam leaves.

Sam smiled and replied, "Good night." He turned on a dime and exited as they watched him. Brianna was not sure he would say yes but if he did, he would be a great addition. But he would have to decide that for himself she surmised.

CHAPTER 21

Adele opened the door. Dillon's head rose, his sulky eyes dropped on Adele's hard face. "Your time is up. We need you to leave the facility," Adele commands, totally ignoring his look.

Dillon blinked at her before a smile crept up along his face. He looked away as Adele stood firm. Adele would prefer he made this easy for her. She needed to be the one to kick him out, this way she would be the one that would call the tip line that would hang him.

She wanted the reward money and besides, she did worry what he would do to Kelvin when this was all over. He can't do much if he was in jail. Dillon stood up. Adele relaxed her shoulders and held her hips in anticipation of what he would say. He said nothing walking towards her. He suddenly stopped and looked down with a frown, Adele did not let herself get caught up in his gaze. Cutting her eyes, she twirled and walked forward. She could hear the chomp of his boots on the floor behind her.

She instantly stepped to the side and waved her hand forward allowing him to lead the way. She did not trust this man. Dillon walked in front of her without a word, while Adele followed him closely. They walked silently.

Adele wondered how much money it would be. It better be a lot. She was not looking to rat him out for some small reward. She really should have checked how much it was. But she had been busy dealing with all the chaos. In a way she enjoyed it. But it can get too much sometimes. Adele really hoped Brianna rethinks the no salary thing.

Adele groaned inwardly knowing she won't. Adele will have to get money through other means like she always did. She led Dillon out of the building. They walked side by side down the steps to the sidewalk.

"Don't try and come back. You won't be able to get in," Adele told him.

Dillion was in front of her, he did not even turn around when she said it, "I might not be able to get back in. But he's gonna come out sometime."

This annoying little…

"Whatever. Get out of here," Adele replied. Dillon started to walk away from the building. Adele watched Dillon walk down the sidewalk.

Adele heaved a sigh of relief. Her body shivered to the chilling atmosphere. She was a bit under clothed for this cold night but it will be warmer when she was covered with the reward money. Once she noticed he was down the sidewalk out of ear range, Adele pulled out her cellphone. She dialed the number she saw back then.

Adele waited for the other end of the line to answer.

It clicked. "Yes. I have a location for a local wanted man..."

CHAPTER 22

Brianna stood just outside of the room looking in as Angelic watched over April who was shooting heroin once again.

"I can't wait till I don't have to do this to function," April said.

Angelic replied, "I know honey. You'll get there. We're all going to make sure you make it. Bri won't let you fail."

They both didn't know Brianna was just outside the doorway. She doesn't want them to know, so she walked away quietly.

She decided to visit Kelvin to know how he was doing. Brianna went into his room as noiseless as she could be. Softly she walked to Kevin's bedside. Kelvin noticed her suddenly, his eyes following her.

"Hey," Brianna said.

"Hey," he replied.

"You doing alright?"

"I am now." His eyebrow curved upward, "Is he gone?"

"Yeah. He won't be coming back. For as long as you're here with us you'll be safe."

"For real this time?"

"For real. You have my word."

Kelvin nodded; his face filled with relief. It was like all his troubles were gone. Brianna worked towards that end and was glad he felt safe now. She knew the streets were unforgiving just like Dillon.

"Can I ask you something?" Kelvin asked knocking Brianna out of her thoughts.

"Sure."

Kelvin hesitated, his hand moving about awkwardly as if struggling to find the words. He sighed, then he asked. "Why do you do this? I don't have insurance. I don't come from a nice neighborhood. People see me as a gang member." He looked away, "Worthless. So why help me?"

"Cause it's the right thing to do. Cause other people see you exactly the way you said."

He looked at her as he asked, "And you don't?"

"I see you just as another person. I could be where you are in a blink of an eye. If that were to happen, I'd hope someone would be there for me. Not see me as someone with or without insurance. Not as a resident of this or that neighborhood. Not as a gang member. Nurse. Teacher. Homeless person. Just a person. That's really all we are. Just people."

Kelvin smiled, leaning back, her reply made him feel so good. He hadn't felt that way in years.

CHAPTER 23

The sirens were blaring, Dillion screeched to a stop as the other cars surrounded him. The storm of police vehicles had him shook, he tried to turn but the cops grabbed him easily sending him to the ground.

Officers quickly detained Dillon and walked him towards the back of one police van.

Detective Gray watched them, taking his time the officer read him his Miranda rights. Detective Gray made his move. He walked at the open door, a big smile on his face.

"Hello, Mr. Brown. How are you feeling?" Detective Gray asked. Dillon stopped, gave Him a blank but intense glare.

"Bite me," Dillon replied, giving Gray a death stare.

"Going on a friendly stroll? Where'd you come from? Where you headed?"

Dillon didn't say anything as he was placed in the back of the police car.

"Guess we'll talk later," Gray said, a smirk on his face as he shut the door.

STREET NURSE

TO BE CONTINUED…..